DEATH IN THE SERENGETI AND OTHER STORIES

TEN TALES OF CRIME

DAVID H. HENDRICKSON

PENTUCKET PUBLISHING

Death in the Serengeti and Other Stories

"Looking for the Bastard" originally appeared in *Pulphouse Fiction Magazine*, Issue #1, edited by Dean Wesley Smith, WMG Publishing Inc., January 2018

"Huram's Temple" originally appeared in *Ellery Queen's Mystery Magazine*, March/April 2015, edited by Janet Hutchings.

"The Kids Keep Coming" originally appeared in *Fiction River: Tavern Tales*, edited by Kerrie L. Hughes, WMG Publishing, Inc., January 2017

"City of Sin Strangler" originally appeared in *Fiction River: Editor Saves*, edited by Kristine Kathryn Rusch, WMG Publishing, Inc., August 2018

"In Another Life" originally appeared in *Flash Me Magazine*, Vol. 6, Issue 21, 2008

"Death in the Serengeti" originally appeared in *Fiction River: Pulse Pounders: Adrenaline*, edited by Kevin J. Anderson, WMG Publishing, Inc., July 2017

ISBN-13: 978-1-948134-09-5
ISBN-10: 1-948134-09-8

The smell of newly rotting flesh hit Jakaya Makinda. He stopped his Land Rover, grabbed his binoculars off the seat beside him, and trained them in the direction of the odor's source.

Eighty meters away, mostly hidden by a rocky outcropping of man-sized boulders, lay the carcasses of a dozen or more slaughtered elephants.

Poachers.

PRAISE FOR DAVID H. HENDRICKSON

"['Death in the Serengeti' has] great setting, instantly engaging peril for the character...a definite Pulse Pounder."

– *New York Times* bestselling author
Kevin J. Anderson

"Michael Connelly's Harry Bosch is perhaps my favorite fictional detective. So the moment I understood Hendrickson's 'detective' Nora O'Sullivan [in 'City of Sin Strangler'] embodies Bosch's principle of 'everybody counts or nobody counts,' you can guarantee she'll be a character I can get behind fully. The story contains a gritty and tragic element of revenge married with a startling and unexpected choice that nobody would ever want to make. It is a story that still gives me a delightful shiver."

– Mark Leslie, author of *Evasion*

"David H. Hendrickson is one of my favorite writers."

– Edgar-nominated author
Kris Nelscott

"Loved the story."

– *Tangent Online,* "Looking for the Bastard"

To Mary Winston McCarriston,
My great friend and unofficial publicist.
Thank you for your boundless enthusiasm for my work.

CONTENTS

INTRODUCTION

In the beginning, I wanted to write like Harlan Ellison. The first story of his that I read, "The Beast That Shouted Love at the Heart of the World," ignited my desire to become a writer. A day later, I started scribbling my first paragraphs.

As I read more and more of Ellison's spectacular works, I became more and more inspired. And intimidated. And overwhelmed at the magnificence of stories like "The Whimper of Whipped Dogs," "Paladin of the Lost Hour," and "Jeffty is Five."

Ah, "Jeffty is Five." If the Devil had come along and in exchange for my soul offered me the ability to write a story anything close to its equal, I wouldn't have stood a chance.

So I tried to write like Harlan Ellison. Which was (and is) impossible. I tried to capture that passion, emotion, empathy, style, wit, and more than anything, that sense of perfect reality even within a story of the fantastic. I failed miserably, of course.

I didn't consider writing any other genre even though I had found the masters of mystery and suspense: John D. MacDonald's Travis McGee series, Robert B. Parker's

Spenser novels (in my own Bostonian back yard, no less), Ed McBain's 87th Precinct series, and so many more. I equated mystery and suspense to novels—I hadn't yet found the mystery digest magazines—and I...did...not...write...novels.

Anytime I did muster the courage to try writing a novel, by the time I got to page fifty—if I even got that far—I would go back and read in horror and despair what I'd produced. It was always utterly wretched. (Trust me on this one. *Utterly wretched.* Totally unreadable. There is no room for dissenting opinion here.)

I would conclude yet again that I had no talent and I was wasting my time. Sometimes I would go back to short stories. More often, I'd quit writing entirely. What was the point? I was hideous! Months would pass before writing inevitably coaxed me back.

Come back into my arms, writing would call to me, *and let me crush your spirit all over again.*

I'd return to writing short stories (having once again sworn off novels forever) because the passion still burned. Yeah, that passion just would not go away. Even if, as lovers went, writing was as heartless as they come. The ultimate in unrequited love. Even if for the longest time my short stories sucked, too.

I kept at it. Mostly doing everything wrong, unintentionally holding myself back. But I kept at it. Over time, my craft *finally* began to improve, inch by painful inch. I still couldn't give my stories away, but they were a stronger level of unpublishable. Some were humorous—as in I was trying to make people laugh, as opposed to they were laughing at me —but otherwise they remained stories of the fantastic.

Like Harlan's.

Except for that quality thing. Except for anyone ever wanting to read them.

It wasn't until I fell under the ever-so-fortunate tutelage of Kristine Kathryn Rusch and Dean Wesley Smith—the two mentors to whom I owe my writing career—that I began to write in other genres. Cautiously at first, but with increasing frequency and enthusiasm. And also with increasing levels of skill. (I even attempted novels, completed them, and sold them! But that's another story for another time.)

Eventually, I found my instincts pointing me to mystery and suspense first, not last. What had once been the rare exception became my default. *Ellery Queen's Mystery Magazine* bought and published "Huram's Temple." *Pulphouse* did the same for "Looking for the Bastard," as did *Fiction River* for "City of Sin Strangler," "The Kids Keep Coming," and my biggest breakthrough of all, "Death in the Serengeti." You'll find all those stories between these covers.

Now, I feel that my best work is in this field. It's taken me a long, long time to get here, but mystery and suspense feels like home.

—David H. Hendrickson
Boston, MA
March 14, 2019

LOOKING FOR THE BASTARD

INTRODUCTION TO "LOOKING FOR THE BASTARD"

This is the only story I've ever written inspired by a piece of art.

I've heard accounts from the pulp era of writers rushing to science fiction magazine offices as soon as they heard the new batch of cover art had arrived. They'd then pitch the story they would write to match the cover, improvising as they went along, and hope for the assignment. A writer getting to the offices too late—after all the good, or at least passable, pieces had been taken—would have to somehow conjure feigned inspiration upon viewing the worst of the worst, the art no one else wanted anything to do with, and come up with *something* that would get them the assignment.

Hey, it's what writers did in that era to be able to pay the rent and buy the groceries. No doubt, I'd have gone hungry. Not exactly the quickest thinker on my feet anyway, I never could have improvised a story idea while staring at an alien blob or whatever else passed for the worst of the worst art in that era. Perhaps I just haven't tried it enough, but I don't get story ideas from art.

With this one exception.

I'd gotten an assignment to write for an anthology with the theme of "stolen." The story could be of any genre, but it had to hit that theme. At about the same time, I saw a haunting photograph of a train station taken by my talented high school friend Matt Muise (www.matthewmuisephotography.com). The train station was in the downtown section of the tough, gritty city we grew up in, Lynn, Massachusetts (of "Lynn, Lynn, City of Sin" fame).

As someone who took the late train many a time from Lynn back into school in Boston, I can attest to that station having an ominous feel to it even without Matt's special-effects magic. All those decades ago, I felt certain it was only a matter of time before I got mugged, no matter how much I tried to portray a badass, don't-mess-with-me persona. (Or as much of a badass persona as a clean-cut, MIT geek could manage.) The mugging never happened, but my pulse rate always eased back to normal when the train doors closed with me inside, heading for the relative safety of Boston. (Yeah, you read that right.)

Matt's magic, however, took an already spooky train station at night, mixed in an eerie glow, and produced a whole new level of dread. You can see it on the e-book cover to this story, recently released as an individual title (www.books2read.com/lookingbastard).

"Looking for the Bastard" was the product of pairing the theme of stolen with Matt's brilliant photograph. As it turned out, the story wasn't quite what the editor of that anthology was looking for, but to my delight it was quickly snapped up by *Pulphouse,* the legendary, recently revived magazine. It became my first of what will be numerous appearances in those revered pages.

LOOKING FOR THE BASTARD

I'm standing on the platform. Alone. Looking for the bastard.

Walked up the twenty-one cracked and crumbling concrete steps to get here from the deserted street below, leaning hard on the rusted, black handrail.

Don't see nothing, other than the usual: crushed-out cigarette butts, white-splattered pigeon droppings, a crumpled bag from McDonald's, and a used condom over near the graffiti-covered cement wall.

The place smells of urine. Maybe my own sweat, too. It was hot today, almost ninety and humid. I ain't had a good, hot shower in a while. Ain't had a good meal in a while, neither.

But I pay that no mind.

'Cause I'm looking for the bastard.

Looking for him through a darkness broken only by the haunting glow cast by the floodlights spaced fifty feet apart, humming their high-pitched tune above my mostly bald, black head. Further off down the platform, at the end where the floodlights can't quite penetrate the darkness and the weeds poke out of the concrete cracks, rats squeal.

My tired bones creak as I move my scrawny ass in little more than a shuffle toward the dark gray trash bin of my nightmares. Overflowing, it's chained to one of the puke-green pillars that rise to the metal overhang above, an overhang that sounds like drum beats when it rains. The trash bin smells of its garbage, not quite ripe but still garbage. I poke about, but see nothing.

I scratch the gray whiskers on my face and move closer to the tracks. I look across to the red-brick three-story factory building a couple hundred feet away, but no lights are on. I look down at the tracks to make sure the bastard ain't down there, the toes of my scuffed and tattered brown shoes on the three-inch-wide, yellow caution line. But he ain't there.

Caution.

Now that's a word for ya.

———

SOME WHO DON'T UNDERSTAND what it's like for people like us say we shouldn't ever play the lottery. Should spend that money on food and rent and clothes and shoes for our feet. They may have a point, but they don't know what it's like to have no hope, to be like a drowning man whose head finally pokes above water, but before he even gets a chance to gulp so much as a single breath of air, a large wave or a strong, hateful hand slams him back under.

That's what I felt like back before everything changed. On the wait list for a place in the projects cause we couldn't afford the rent. A trip to the grocery store didn't never get no cheaper. And little Angie, our only child, a sweet nine-year-old girl who wouldn't hurt a fly, seemed to outgrow her clothes fast as we could buy them, and not just cause she was chubby. And when she needed the medicine, it was like taking my whole paycheck and flushing it down the toilet.

Ain't like we was spending our money on trips to A-ruba.

So every now and then, I'd spend a dollar I shouldn'ta spent on a lottery ticket. I knew I shouldn't, but I couldn't help myself. I just needed a little bit of hope, you know?

Hope that I'd actually bust out of that overwhelming wave and actually get to breathe.

And you know what? The most blessed miracle ever came down from Heaven above.

Or so I thought.

I won! Over six hundred and fifty thousand dollars!

Six hundred and fifty...*thousand*...dollars.

Course I coulda taken it in something they called an annuity where they'd pay me a little each year, but a man like me who's been lied to and cheated what feels like every day of his life ain't taking no annuity.

Give me the cash money and let me breathe, man, let me breathe!

I tell you, there was a lot of tears in our kitchen the night I brought home that check and showed it to my wife, Gerty —a thin, tired-looking woman with an almost constant look of sadness in her eyes—and then to Angie. Gerty certainly didn't look tired anymore and that look of sadness in her eyes was gone. I don't know if I ever seen her happier, except the day Angie was born. We was all crying and laughing and jumping up and down for joy.

'Specially Angie. Her mother, and other busybodies who can't seem to mind their own business, would tell her not to be so loud all the time. Shush, girl. Tone it down. You embarrassing.

But her mother wasn't telling Angie to tone it down that night even as that little butterball of sweetness whooped it up as loud as a jet airplane taking off.

Whoo-ee. Our joy was complete.

I was half a mind to go down to the plant and tell the super—a white man named Joe Gordon who'd walk over his momma and grandma, too, just to get ahead, and who hadn't minded walking all over the likes of me—that he could take his goddamned job and stick it somewhere.

But I ain't stupid.

Six hundred and fifty thousand dollars is a lot of money, a whole lot more than just a life preserver tossed to this drowning man, but not enough to live on for the rest of your life. Not even if you're single, much less a man with a wife and a nine-year-old girl.

So I wasn't going to be a fool and quit my job or be a real damned fool and punch that Joe Gordon right in the nose, like he deserved. I was still gonna show up each day, put in my time, and keep collecting that paycheck.

I might have a whole different goddamned attitude, I'll tell you that. A *whole* different goddamned attitude. But I wasn't gonna get myself fired or nothing stupid like that. I was gonna mind my business and take care of business.

And that's exactly what I did.

Didn't even let that damned Joe Gordon know I won six hundred and fifty thousand dollars, though he found out—word gets around about that sort of thing—and he kinda looked at me different for a while there, as if he was expecting me to punch him in the mouth like he deserved.

But I was smart. I was finally able to breathe the air about me. And even if it wasn't no sweet mountain air or no rich Beverly Hills air with the smell of chlorine in the pools and rose bushes and bark mulch in the flower bed, it was air.

Gritty, dirty city air, but air.

I could breathe.

Until Angie disappeared and the bastard left his ransom note in our mail slot.

Hey Rich Man,

If you ever want to see your little girl again, be near your phone at 7:30 tonight for the next directions.

NO COPS! If I even think I see one of them, I'll cut your little girl open like a plump Thanksgiving Day turkey.

———

Took a long time to get the six hundred thousand in cash. Not the full six hundred and fifty thousand. The bastard, his voice coarse and distorted over the phone, had laughed and said he assumed I'd spent fifty grand already, a fool like me always does that, and if I hadn't, wasn't he a nice guy leaving me all that dough?

So I bought me a briefcase, a cheap one, dark brown with no lock—never had reason to own a briefcase before that— and I packed all that money in it. Had Gerty drive me to the train station. We didn't say nothing. Didn't look at each other.

Didn't have to.

Couldn't.

Just sat in the darkness of the car down below the station, parked along the curbside, and waited, looking up at it every few seconds, our hearts pounding even while they were breaking. Sweat formed on our foreheads, the air heavy and warm. My fists clenched and unclenched. Beside me, Gerty softly sobbed.

The 9:58 p.m. train arrived in a whoosh of air, noisy and screeching. What felt like several lifetimes later, it left. Several lifetimes after that, a couple emerged from the concrete stairwell and walked the couple hundred yards down the street to the commuter parking lot.

Several lifetimes after that, I walked up the twenty-one stairs alone, the briefcase in one hand and the plastic bag of trash I'd brought, following the bastard's directions, in the other. They felt like they weighed a couple hundred tons, but that was nothing compared to how heavy my heart felt.

Not because I cared about the money.

Oh, I cared about the money, all right. There was six hundred *thousand* dollars inside that briefcase, after all. That money had let me breathe, given me hope for our family's future.

Angie's future. She could get her crooked teeth fixed. She could go to college. Be something more than her father, just a poor, dumb laborer at the plant who got lucky with a couple numbers on a ticket.

She could be anything.

But it was turning out that money wasn't going to let me breathe. Wasn't going to let my little girl get her teeth fixed or go to college and make something out of herself. This drowning man had gotten his couple gulps of air, but now a hateful, cruel hand was thrusting him down beneath the waves one last time, this one for good.

So much for luck.

All I wanted now was to get my little girl back. To hell with the goddamned money, just so long as I got Angie back. So I'd said nothing to the police. Didn't trust them to protect my little girl. I'd seen too many things in my lifetime to trust them at all.

So I was on my own. Nobody but me up here and Gerty down in the car.

I was alone here on the platform, but the bastard had to be here or nearby somewhere. Had to be watching me somehow, perhaps from a window in the old, red-brick three-story factory building on the other side of the tracks set back a few hundred feet. No lights shone in any of the windows, but I knew the bastard had to be in there somewhere.

Watching me go to the chained trash bin, now only half filled with trash. Place the loaded suitcase into the trash bin and cover it with the plastic bag of my own trash.

I looked over at the factory building and pointed to the trash bin, sure he was watching. I touched a hand to my heart, and clasped my hands in a begging gesture.

Then I went back down to the car, nodded quick to Gerty, who looked away and broke into gasping sobs even as tears streaked down my own face.

And we waited for first the 10:14 train, and then the 10:43 to arrive.

The 10:43. The train that was supposed to have Angie aboard. Making no sense at all, I thought of how that was after her bedtime. As if that mattered at all now.

We were told to stay away until that train arrived and we did. No one entered or left the station for the 10:14, and no one came to wait for the 10:43.

As soon as we heard the train rumbling down the tracks and clanging to announce its arrival, we bolted from the car, not locking it, not even thinking to slam shut the doors. We shot up those twenty-one stairs, ignoring the black handrail, and were there waiting long before the train came to a screeching halt.

Of course, Angie didn't step off that train and run crying into our arms.

Of course, the suitcase full of money was gone, the plastic bag of trash left behind.

And of course, of course, of course, Angie's lifeless body was found days later in a dumpster behind a Burger King.

In a goddamned dumpster. My little girl.

———

WE WAS on the TV news for two days. Mostly about how what fools we'd been not to trust the police, or the FBI if it had come to that, to get our Angie back. The TV reporters shook their heads at our stupidity, and how now the odds were stacked against finding the killer. And on one station, a newscaster raised an eyebrow at what a man like me was doing buying a lottery ticket in the first place.

Then the world forgot us.

For us, it was almost a blessing, but I couldn't help thinking about JonBenet whatshername with her pretty face, curly blonde hair, and beauty-pageant smile. She got kidnapped and killed just like Angie—unless her parents killed her, of course—but while everyone has forgotten about Angie, JonBenet whatshername lives on in TV movies and shows, twenty, twenty-five years after her death.

I know why ain't no one gonna do a TV movie about Angie. She wasn't a cute, white girl with pretty blonde hair. Angie was a big, black girl, and the TV don't like big, black girls unless they on daytime TV shows about cheating boyfriends and paternity tests, and even then the TV just making fun of those girls. Any fool knows that. No, my Angie wasn't gonna be in no beauty pageants like that JonBenet whatshername.

But the TV oughta remember my girl 'cause her laughter, even if it was too loud, could warm a house with no heat in the dead of winter. She had a sweetness I bet that JonBenet couldn't hold a candle to.

And that bastard snuffed that laughter and sweetness out.

All because of that damned six hundred and fifty thousand dollars. The day doesn't go by that I don't regret buying that damned lottery ticket.

Maybe it isn't that big a deal that the world has forgotten about Angie. If it remembered her, that wouldn't bring her back. If it remembered her, that wouldn't bring my Gerty back either, Gerty who finally couldn't take it no more and swallowed the entire bottle of the sleeping pills her doctor had prescribed.

The bastard took it all away.

And so I'm alone. Whether it's at our empty apartment —*my* empty apartment—or up on the elevated platform of that train station, I'm alone.

That's why I keep looking for the bastard who stole away my little girl. Who stole away my life. I figure he'll come back to the scene of his crime some day.

And I'll catch him. I don't know exactly what I'll do when that happens, but I sure have given it a lot of thought.

So every night when the 9:58 train is about to come rumbling and clanging into the station, I climb those twenty-one stairs, their concrete a little more cracked and crumbling each time, the black handrail a little more rusted.

It's been almost thirty years now that I've been coming here.

Thirty years. Every night.

Looking for the bastard.

SLEEPYVILLE, USA

INTRODUCTION TO "SLEEPYVILLE, USA"

From the mean streets of Lynn to the sleepy suburbs. Crime doesn't always sleep in the 'burbs, but it sure is a lot more quiet. Until it isn't.

In "Sleepyville, USA," I wanted to look at a cop who seems to have a cushy job compared to his big city compatriots, but must rise to the challenge when murder comes to his quiet, little town.

SLEEPYVILLE, USA

WHEN YOU'RE A cop, you never *expect* to get a call for a murder. You don't look at your watch and say, "It's nine o'clock, no dead bodies yet?" and then tap the watch to make sure it's working right. You never *expect* it.

But when the call comes, you might feel only slump-shouldered resignation.

Or eye-blinking, dry-mouthed, cold sweat shock.

———

JIMMY FLANAGAN FLIPPED on the siren and broke into a cold sweat. He'd been listening to WOKQ, New Hampshire's giant country music station, and sipping his Dunkin' Donuts coffee—hazelnut, black with two Splendas, and so hot that curls of steam still rose from its surface—when the call came in. He'd begun to wonder if perhaps Chris O'Rourke, a Boston cop and an old Melrose High School buddy, had been right.

Chris had said that Sleepyville, USA—his nickname for

Fernville, New Hampshire— had turned Jimmy into nothing but a soft marshmallow. The streets he patrolled in this one-stoplight town were tree-lined, the maples full and green now that spring was in full bloom, and dotted with businesses like Village Subs and Pizza, Mrs. B's Breakfast Nook and Luncheon, Fernville Pharmacy, and Caldwell's Famous Antiques.

The streets Chris patrolled were blood-stained, populated with boarded-up three-story houses long since condemned, warring gangs, and whores who would sell their souls for their next hit. Jimmy's beat moved to the music of Lee Greenwood's "God Bless the USA," Chris's to Eminem's "Kill You." Chris had been spry and nimble on his feet when he'd captained and quarterbacked the Melrose High football team and he remained that way today. He had to. Jimmy had played little as a second-string linebacker, already too thick about the middle to move quickly, and thicker still today. He could get away with it.

"How many times you gotten shot at?" Chris asked. "I bet you only got shot at once or twice."

Jimmy had been all set to lie and say he'd been shot at twice, even though it hadn't ever happened even once, but Chris had denied him even the lie.

"You ain't been shot even once," Chris said, shaking his head in amazement at Jimmy's soft, cushy life.

"I didn't say that."

"You didn't need to. You're even easier to read than the dumbest perp on my beat. And I got some really dumb ones."

"I've gotten shot at," Jimmy said. "Put your pistol back in your pants. You ain't half as smart as you think you are."

Chris had raised an eyebrow and said no more.

But now Jimmy, his mouth as dry as cotton with the

coffee aftertaste now bitter on his tongue, wondered if Chris had been right. Jimmy's gut churned with the fear that still lurked even after fifteen years on the job and would remain there until the day he retired.

He *was* soft, soft as a marshmallow. He'd never had to dodge a bullet, or solve even a single murder or rape.

Soft.

Now he was breaking into a cold sweat, that raw, sour taste in his mouth, all because he'd finally caught a call that sounded like a bad one.

—————

DELORES PRESCOTT WAVED WILDLY from behind her silver Ford Focus, puffing hard on a cigarette, its tip glowing. She'd parked near the end of the Elmwood Estates cul-de-sac just before the circular turnabout, blocking in its driveway a familiar Chevy Malibu with the vanity plate PROF.

William Stackhouse's car. William, not Bill or Billy. About fifty years old or so. A former instructor for twenty-some years at the prestigious Philips Exeter Preparatory School in neighboring Exeter a dozen or so miles away. A bit of a stuffed shirt, "full of himself" according to some of the locals, but not a bad guy, Jimmy thought.

A thickly wooded forest stretched behind the fifteen houses that lined the cul-de-sac, only a few bought by old-timers like William Stackhouse, the rest by Massholes, as the locals called them, new money and arrogant attitudes that had migrated up from Massachusetts.

Jimmy killed the siren and radioed back to the station, but left the blue flashers going. Curious faces stared out from behind windows or partly opened front doors. Sprinklers sprayed water across the freshly cut lawns and birds called from the deepening forest beyond the backyards. Further in the distance, a woodpecker hammered.

Jimmy climbed out of the patrol car, hitched up his pants, and wiped the clammy sweat off his forehead. Delores ground the butt of her cigarette, a Salem if Jimmy remembered correctly, underfoot.

Delores, reeking of the smoke, looked as if she was about to faint. "It's awful. The worstest thing I ever saw." Her voice was that of a long-time smoker, husky and gravelly. "I came here to talk to Gladys. Gladys Stackhouse, don't you know. It's her husband...." Delores pointed at the Malibu, wobbled, then coughed a harsh, hacking cough and wheezed in a big gulp of air. "We were working on the Women's Missionary Council event coming up at the church next month. Me and Gladys, I mean." She shook her head. "Now he's dead. Her husband. William Stackhouse. Somebody kilt him."

Jimmy glanced at the Malibu and reflexively touched his holster. Out of the corner of his eye, he saw Delores flinch. *What did she think, he was going to shoot her? What's wrong with these people?* Even after living here for fifteen years, it was still him, the newcomer, and "these people," all the old Yankees who didn't quite trust anyone whose parents their own parents hadn't gone to school with. They viewed him the same way he viewed the Massholes.

Jimmy surveyed the surrounding houses and made a mental note of the heads looking out the windows and those standing in full view on their porches: Carl Gunderson, arms folded, at his dark brown ranch; Rachel Merriweather at her white Colonial, craning her neck for a better view; and figures at two houses he couldn't make out and couldn't recall the residents' names.

People talked about rubbernecking as if it only happened with highway accidents, but Jimmy knew better. A siren and the flashing blue lights drew crowds everywhere.

He realized belatedly that a sense of calm had come over him, perhaps because of Delores's panic or perhaps because he felt no imminent danger or perhaps because he'd forgotten that a dead body awaited him in the car less than ten paces away.

"When did you find him?" Jimmy asked. Delores fumbled another Salem out of its pack—he'd remembered correctly—and lit it with shaking hands.

"Right before I called," she said, fixing him with an annoyed aren't-you-dumber-than-a-rock look. "Don't you know when that was? Don't you folks keep records?"

"Yeah, we do."

"Did you think I'd let a dead body just sit there?" She coughed another raspy, hacking cough. "Jesus, Jimmy, what kind of fool do you take me for? I watch TV."

He began to walk toward the Malibu, feeling the calm slipping away and a sense of dread slide up over him like a shroud, starting at his suddenly unsteady feet and slipping up, up, up, until it covered his face. He could breathe in only his own sour, warm exhalations and then he couldn't breathe in anything at all.

Chris O'Rourke had been right. Soft as a marshmallow.

Avoiding the urge to place a hand on the Malibu to steady himself, Jimmy peered through the window. For a moment, he saw only his own reflection and began to fumble inside his pants pocket for a handkerchief to open the door with. Then the reflection cleared and Jimmy saw William Stackhouse all too clearly.

He sat slumped over the steering wheel, his face twisted

sideways, eyes bulging out and mouth wide open as if shocked to see Jimmy and Delores. *Don't look at me*, he seemed to be saying. *Not like this.* A screwdriver, looking gleaming and new, protruded out of his neck. Blood, now dried, had leaked from the corners of his mouth and splattered the dashboard and the front of his yellow Izod polo shirt.

In the distance, the ambulance's siren droned, but Jimmy knew it need not bother. There'd be no race to the hospital for William Stackhouse.

AFTER JIMMY RADIOED in and called off the ambulance and summoned the county medical examiner, he returned to Delores, who'd gone through two more cigarettes while she waited.

"Is she inside?" Jimmy asked. "Does she know?"

"Who, Gladys? No." Delores glanced at her watch. "I was a little early. That's how I am. I believe in being punctual. More than punctual." She said the word punctual as if she'd just learned it out of a self-improvement book and was showing off. "Gladys isn't always punctual. She has many fine qualities, I'll grant you, but being punctual isn't one of them." Delores pursed her lips. "She's late today."

"So she doesn't know yet?"

Delores gave him the dumb-as-rocks look again. "No."

In the silence that followed, the next door lawn sprinkler's *thwack-thwack-thwack* seemed to grow a few decibels. The smell of the freshly cut grass through Delores's lingering cigarette smell.

"Had you observed any tension between Gladys and William?" Jimmy asked.

Again, the look. "Are you asking if they were a couple out of one of them trashy romance novels the Catholics like to read? No. That isn't how life is. It isn't how marriage is. That's the problem with young girls these days. They think marriage is going to be easy. All flowers and pretty sunsets and...what's the word they use? *Soulmates.*" Delores practically spat it out. "Do a man's dirty laundry for thirty years and then talk to me about soulmates. Ain't no such thing." She coughed. "So no, they weren't *soulmates.* But they didn't hate each other neither. In the middle like everyone else. Bored and distant but putting up with it." She eyed Jimmy. "She didn't kill William, if that's what you're asking, and I know that's what you're asking. She didn't do this. She couldn't have done this. Not Gladys."

GLADYS STACKHOUSE PULLED up to the scene minutes later in her beat-up Chevy Corsica and leapt out of the car without even pulling over to the side. She ran to Jimmy, a big woman, close to two hundred pounds in an unflattering black-and-white print dress, looking all of her fifty or so years. Her eyes grew wide and her face froze in panic.

"*What happened?*"

Jimmy took her by the elbow and led her away from the body. He could almost smell the raw intensity of her fear. She shook all over.

"*What happened?*" She looked into Jimmy's eyes and began to cry. "*Jimmy? Is he...?*"

Jimmy nodded. "I'm sorry. I'm very sorry." This task had been forced on him before, almost always the result of an automobile or motorcycle accident, but it never got easy. The violence inflicted on William Stackhouse's body made it somehow worse. A closer inspection had shown that the screwdriver hung from the second of two stabbings of the throat. "Mrs. Stackhouse, your husband has been killed."

She collapsed in his arms, dead weight, smelling faintly of perspiration and onions, and Jimmy had all he could do to keep her head from smacking the pavement and cracking open like a ripe melon. At times like this, he thought, being a little too thick around the middle wasn't a bad thing.

———

"DID YOUR HUSBAND HAVE ANY ENEMIES?" Jimmy asked Gladys Stackhouse much later. They sat at the Stackhouse dining room table, surrounded by hundreds of ornate China dolls, some atop the surface of a mahogany cabinet and within a matching hutch and others on shelves.

Gladys had brewed coffee—Dunkin' Donuts hazelnut, in fact—and Jimmy sniffed the aroma like a fine wine and gratefully sipped the steaming liquid.

"No one who would do that to him," Gladys said, shuddering. She touched her index finger and thumb to her lips and looked about to cry. Her makeup was smudged, her bright red lipstick smeared.

"We can do this later," Jimmy said, although he hoped she'd continue. He couldn't imagine that she'd done it. Nobody could be that good of an actress. But something nagged at him.

"No," she said. "Let's get this over with."

"Any recent arguments?"

"No." She looked up in surprise. "Do you mean with me?"

"With anyone." He sipped his coffee and looked for a reaction.

"No."

Something bothered Jimmy about the tone in Gladys's response. He'd come back to the question.

"William did tutoring, right? SAT prep. That sort of thing?"

"Yes. Well, all kinds of tutoring really. He was a very smart man. SAT preparation like you said, but also individual tutoring in just about every subject. Over at the prep and at Durham."

"The prep" was local terminology for Philips Exeter, the prep school where William Stackhouse had taught for more than two decades, and Durham was the main campus for the University of New Hampshire.

"He spends a lot of time at both campuses. He's very much in demand." Her face fell. "I mean...he *was* very much in demand."

"Could a student have become upset with him after doing poorly?"

"I suppose it's possible, but he's really very good. Was really very good. Most students recognize that he's given them all the tools to succeed. If they fail, it's because they didn't apply themselves."

Jimmy nodded. "Are you sure he'd had no recent arguments with anyone?"

"No, nothing recent." Her eyes shifted.

Jimmy tapped a finger on the table. "What happened that wasn't recent?"

"Nothing. It was just...it was a figure of speech. I mean, if he got in a schoolyard fight forty years ago, would that count?"

Jimmy tapped again. "I don't think so."

"Neither did I."

"What happened that wasn't recent?"

"Nothing." She took in a deep breath. "I think that's as much as I can handle right now. Can I get you a fresh cup for the road?"

Jimmy waited a few seconds, then got out of his chair. "That won't be necessary. Thank you for this." He hefted the empty cup and handed it to her. "And thank you for your time. You know where to reach me if you think of anything."

He thought he'd be back here sooner or later.

IT WAS SOONER. Just hours later that very same afternoon, sitting at the same dining room table, sipping more of the same coffee. Gladys Stackhouse had fixed her makeup but looked far more jittery, rubbing her hands together and glancing nervously at the door.

"Is something wrong?" Jimmy said, then realizing how foolish that sounded, added, "I mean beyond your husband's death."

"No!" She said it more sharply, he thought, than she'd intended. "No." She glanced again to the front door. "I just wanted to let you know...because you were asking...about, you know." She looked at her hands. "A long time ago."

"When?"

"It's really nothing. It can't possibly matter. I shouldn't have called."

"I need to know everything so I can find who did this to your husband."

"It's nothing. I was being silly. Really." She glanced toward the front door. "My mind isn't thinking right anymore. I'm sorry I called you out here."

Jimmy let the silence lie. A clock on the wall ticked and tocked, sounding louder and louder. He sat back in his chair, uncomfortable but hoping to make her feel it even more. He sipped his coffee.

He watched a bead of sweat form on Gladys's forehead. She licked her lips. Swallowed. Smiled weakly.

"It was five years ago," she said, exasperated. "Petty stuff five years ago. It was nothing."

Jimmy calculated. That would have been about the time Stackhouse left the Prep. Jimmy said nothing. He waited.

Gladys exhaled loudly through her nose. "I don't know why, but there were people over at the Prep that were very upset when he left. They acted as though he had betrayed them."

"Betrayed them?"

"Yes. It was silly. He was free to pursue his other opportunities. It's a free country. If they wanted to keep him, they should have paid him more. Tutoring pays better than teaching. Not at the beginning. It takes a while to establish yourself. But eventually. I never could understand it and it upset William so much he wouldn't discuss it."

Jimmy had to agree with Gladys. It had been nothing. She had been wasting his time. To think that some academic would murder a former colleague over some dispute from five years ago seemed absurd.

"Anything else?" Jimmy asked.

Gladys shook her head. "No, that's it."

"Could you show me where your husband kept his business records?"

Gladys averted her eyes. "I'm not sure."

"You're not sure where his records are?"

"I mean, they're in a file cabinet and on his computer." She brushed a bead of sweat off her forehead.

"I'd like to look at those records."

Gladys didn't say anything. *Tick. Tock. Tick. Tock.*

"Could I take the computer for a few days? And the file cabinet?"

"Why?"

"Because right now the possibility that one of his students did this seems like our best lead." Jimmy tapped on the table hard. "The person who killed him was a very angry man or woman." He tapped again. "The spouse is the first person we always suspect."

"*Me?*"

"Always the first suspect," Jimmy said. "That's why it would be in your interest to let us see those records without making me get a court order." He smiled. "Give us a chance to identify the other suspects."

Gladys got up and poured herself a glass of water. "I don't know."

"We'll get a court order eventually," he said. "There's no reason not to comply unless...there's something you don't want us to see."

Her eyes darted about nervously. Silence hung heavy in the air.

Jimmy spoke the next words slowly, never taking his eyes off hers. "I would also have to charge you with obstruction of justice and tampering with evidence if anything disappeared from those files or off that computer before we got the court order."

Gladys exhaled loudly through her nose. "You'll need a court order."

———

THE NEXT TWO DAYS, Jimmy tried to keep an eye on the

Stackhouse home when he could without being obvious, a difficult task for a house at the end of a cul-de-sac. Gladys had been jittery for a reason beyond her husband's death. He was sure of it.

He also drove over to Philips Exeter. No one would speak to him about William Stackhouse's resignation. The HR head and the chair of the Humanities Department both cited confidentiality agreements—an odd contention if he'd simply resigned—while giving off attitudes that his departure had been far more complex than that and perhaps not voluntary at all.

———

DURING THE FUNERAL, Jimmy watched the entrance to the Stackhouse home from the wooded area on the opposite side of the cul-de-sac, using binoculars. His instincts had told him something was wrong, something beyond what met the eye. Besides, in the big cities, houses of those involved in funerals got burgled all the time. It wouldn't hurt to keep watch on the house.

So Jimmy cut through the forest and, huffing and puffing, climbed a huge tree with a sightline between two houses, giving him a direct view of the Stackhouse entrance. None of the neighbors were around. Presumably they were attending the funeral. Jimmy thought that a partner who could watch the rear—or who could climb trees like a chimpanzee while he watched the rear from the ground—would be nice, but a Sleepyville cop didn't have that luxury. Sticky pitch covered Jimmy's hands; the sweet smell of pine needles and his own sour sweat filled his nostrils.

A black car from the funeral home picked Gladys up, dressed in black dress with a matching veil. Little more than an hour later, an older compact car that he didn't recognize pulled into the driveway. He wrote down the New Hampshire license plate number and zoomed in the binoculars. A young blonde woman, somewhere between sixteen and twenty-six, got out, wearing a yellow T-Shirt, jeans, and a backpack. She glanced around, and headed up the walkway to the front porch, pulling on a pair of gloves. She fished beneath the Welcome mat and then within the potted plants that lined the railing. Angrily, she swatted the last one aside and ran around behind the house.

Jimmy began the climb down from the tree, hand over sticky hand, careful not to lose either his foothold or his grip. He breathed a sigh of relief when his feet touched ground. He ran to the corner of the neighbor's house that gave him the best view, winded after the first forty yards, sweat stinging his eyes. He peered around the corner and caught a glimpse of yellow moving through the house.

Jimmy cut across the street, stopped at her car, and then raced as best he could to the back door of the Stackhouse home and waited flat against the wall.

———

THE WOMAN EMERGED ALMOST twenty minutes later, flew out the door, and froze when Jimmy barked out the command.

"Drop the pack!"

She turned and faced him, her pretty face a mix of shock and anger. She made to toss him the backpack, then darted away.

As she fled around the corner, Jimmy lumbered after her, thankful she'd taken so long inside, but still bellowing in and out loud gasps of air.

She scrambled into her car and froze. Jimmy huffed and puffed to the car, then stood beside the front door holding aloft the keys he'd pulled out of her ignition twenty minutes earlier.

She screamed, *"You...you don't understand. This isn't fair. None of it. It isn't fair."*

"You're arrested," Jimmy replied.

———

IT TOOK MORE than a week to unravel it all. William Stackhouse had been providing more than SAT and individual course preparation to the students at Philips and UNH. He'd become a personal term paper factory, one who charged a little bit more than those on the Internet but one which was untraceable for students with richer parents than most. Small wonder Gladys Stackhouse had resisted turning over her husband's records.

The young woman, named Cindie Kramer, had been the cause of his demise at Philips Exeter. He'd given her an A in a course for certain favors that neither the school nor her parents wanted publicized. A quiet forced resignation pushed William Stackhouse quickly into the world of plagiarism for profit.

And when Cindie Kramer, now a UNH senior, contracted through a friend for a William Stackhouse special in a key course, William Stackhouse got his revenge, deliberately writing a paper so obviously stolen from other sources that she was discovered and expelled one semester from graduation.

Enraged, she'd killed him, but been scared off by Delores Prescott's arrival, forced to wait until the day of the funeral to steal Stackhouse's incriminating records.

SO JIMMY HAD solved the first Fernville murder in the last fifteen years. He thought of his buddy Chris O'Rourke and how this might have just been a solid week's work for Chris, over and done with. Bring on the next.

Jimmy hoped he never saw another.

HURAM'S TEMPLE

INTRODUCTION TO "HURAM'S TEMPLE"

I f the contrast between the mean streets of Lynn and the sleepy suburbs wasn't enough for you, let's go all the way back to Old Testament Israel.

Writers are invariably told to "write what you know." More often than not, that's horrible advice, at least when taken literally. What if you don't know anything about anything? What if what you do know is drop-dead boring? Of even greater importance, what if you'd rather get a root canal than write about the topics that you do know?

When I first started writing, I figured all I knew about was computers and church. (I was a math-and-sciences geek and a preacher's kid.) I knew those topics inside and out, but could think of few more guaranteed to inflict paralyzing boredom. If not in the reader, then certainly in me. And when I added painfully acquired expertise in failure, I had my Holy Trinity of Tedium.

What I'm convinced of now is that writers should write whatever they are passionate about. If you know great gobs of details about something that bores you to tears, you're not going to enjoy writing about it. Do you want to drag yourself to the computer with a sense of dread or a sense of excitement?

Having said that, I must confess to violating that rule several times in years past. When writing two of my earliest published stories, I swallowed the "write what you know" mantra hook, line, and sinker. Faced with time pressure to meet a difficult deadline and an even more important need to differentiate myself from writers far more skilled than I was, I fell back on Old Testament settings.

As a preacher's kid, I read the Bible from cover to cover most every year. Even the really, *really* boring parts. (Leviticus, I'm looking at you!) I'd breathe a sigh of relief when I got out of the Old Testament—at least until I neared Revelations—but that reading gave me a feel for Old Testament settings. I didn't love them, but they had become familiar.

They fit the "write what you know" mantra.

And so I did use the Old Testament in those two early stories, and yes, that familiarity did help me hit the difficult deadlines and I did avoid treading on the same ground covered by other writers. To my shock and euphoric delight, "Beloved" and "Return to the Garden" sold to the DAW anthologies *The Trouble with Heroes* and *Swordplay*, respectively.

Of course, I don't regret those choices at all. The opening line from "Beloved," a tale about the Biblical King David, remains an all-time favorite: *There's nothing like a man holding the severed head of a giant to get a woman in the mood.*

But I use Old Testament settings sparingly. Eventually, I'll have enough of those stories to make an entire collection of them, and I'm sure they'll appeal to a certain group of readers. Many, however, see the words "Old Testament" and roll their eyes, ready to move on to something more exciting.

If you're one of them, I understand. To a certain extent, I'm one of you.

"Huram's Temple" will be your only trip to those ancient, sand-swept landscapes, but I trust you'll find it worth your while. Janet Hutchings, editor of *Ellery Queen's Mystery Magazine*, thought so. It appeared in the March/April 2015 issue.

Trust me, there will be no theology. Only murder.

Relieved?

HURAM'S TEMPLE

I OFTEN WONDER whether the foundry we work in belongs to Huram, the Phoenician, or King Solomon. It was, of course, the king who ordered and paid for its construction, from the furnace and casting pits to the metal-working tools and benches to the stores of copper and tin. It may be the largest bronze foundry in all the world, over fifty paces by fifty paces in size, filled with over a dozen artisans and twenty slaves. The king built it to furnish his great temple with treasures.

But Huram acts as though it is his very own. A man of prodigious girth and self-love, he struts about, issuing orders both to the men he brought with him from Tyre and true Israelites alike. As if no one else has so much as cast a single medal before in our lives. He is the master artist; we are nothing.

"No!" Huram bellows at one of his men. "You've lost the detail! Start all over. Do it again."

I glance at my friend Elam. We exchange knowing looks and his ruddy face glows, and not just from the sweat caused by the blasting heat of the furnace, stoked hot enough to turn the copper and tin molten. Elam's jovial face always glows with an inner radiance, as if all things amuse him. But in this case he has an extra reason to be merry. We have a wager on how often Huram will explode in anger today, and Elam has just taken one step closer to winning.

My eyes turn to Elam's father, Abimael, but he looks angrily away as if telling us to mind our business. Abimael. Ever serious. Ever bowing to the genius of Huram of Tyre. The three of us are the lone Israelites isolated in a den of Phoenicians and their slaves, but Elam and I often feel as separated from his father as if he, too, worships Baal instead of Jehovah, the god of King Solomon and all true Israelites.

The Phoenicians deny the sacrilege, of course, not wanting to spit on the coins given to them by the king for their labors. They say they believe in many gods, including Jehovah, but is that not forbidden by the tablets Moses brought down from the mount, tablets still resting in the Ark of the Covenant? When the temple is complete and it houses the Ark, will not those tablets cry out at the sacrilege of being surrounded by treasures designed by impure hands?

May King Solomon reign a thousand years and ten. But how could he choose a man from Tyre instead of a true Israelite as his master sculptor? Even if his genius towers over all of us. True, Huram's mother is a widow from the tribe of Naphtali, but his father is a Phoenician craftsman. Huram is a man of Tyre, not Jerusalem. How can the works of an uncircumcised man share a temple with the great Ark of the Covenant?

Within the foundry, he acts as if he is a pagan god himself.

"No, fool!" he shouts at another Phoenician. "You've ruined it again!"

Huram rarely shouts at the three of us Israelites, but that's only because he assigns all the most difficult work, all the most interesting pieces, to his own men while treating us as if we have no skills at all. Our stature ranks barely higher than that of the slaves.

All about me, men use their tools, chipping away the molds surrounding hardened casts or adding fine details to the bronze itself. The clanging of the tools fills my ears. Pieces of the molds crash to the ground as they are broken away from the casts. The slaves stoke the furnace. The smell of its intense fire is in the air.

I press soft wax against my mold so it will capture every detail for the bowl I am working on. In my design, a thread winds around and around and then spins off to start another thread that winds its way all the way around the outside of the bowl. An interesting design, but...

The Phoenicians prepare molds for lions and oxen and cherubim. Mine are for bowls.

Sweat pours down my face, dripping off my chin onto my garments, even as my righteous anger remains bottled inside with no avenue of escape. With a rag, I wipe my face and dry my wet hair, though I wonder why. There is no point. The furnace at the center of the foundry radiates heat of such force that every one of us drips sweat all day. The place reeks of it.

Elam is about to pour molten bronze into his mold when the clatter of hoofs sounds outside. As if in unison, we all turn to the entrance, free men and slaves alike. The room, moments before filled with loud clanging, falls silent. It has been days since the last rain; stirred-up dust that makes its way inside will ruin our work.

"Go away!" Huram shouts as he strides toward the entrance, an angry glare on his face. "I command it!"

The clatter of hoofs slows to a halt. Outside, men dismount and trumpets sound. Two voices, one higher than the other, call out, "Make way for Joakim, envoy of the great King Solomon, may he reign a thousand years and ten!"

I set down my mold. What can this mean? I glance at Elam and Abimael, eyebrows raised but receive only shrugs in return. The three of us and the Phoenicians file out. The slaves, looking even more confused than the rest of us, begin to join us until Huram sees them.

"Tend the furnace!" he commands, and struts out ahead of us into the open clearing that surrounds the foundry. A hundred paces to the north, a long row of tents begins and stretches outward. A hundred paces to the east lies the storehouse where the finished objects are kept.

A cooling breeze wafts over our wet skin. I run my fingers through my damp hair and let the air flow over me like cleansing water. Elam sees me and grins.

"Feels good, doesn't it?" he asks softly.

"Be quiet!" Abimael says through clenched teeth.

Two men standing beside sleek black horses hold ceremonial horns at their sides, their attention directed toward a man seated on a carriage drawn by two pale white horses. Joakim, no doubt. Almost as rotund as Huram, Joakim is clad in royal colors and possesses a fair countenance. Following in his wake are six donkeys, all loaded down with large, coarse sacks. When he's drawn to within thirty paces, he commands his driver to stop. He stands.

Dust billows. The odors of the animals carry downwind to me; I'm not the only one to notice. Elam grimaces in comic overreaction and his father hisses at us both.

Joakim clears his throat and puffs out his chest. "I send greetings from the great King Solomon," he says. "He anxiously awaits the fruits of your labor. They shall make his temple beyond compare."

Joakim smiles at us. I wonder if we are supposed to cheer.

"The king has spared no expense," he continues, "summoning the great master Huram from the land of Tyre."

Huram puffs out his chest and smiles smugly. I want to strike him. Even Abimael looks annoyed.

Joakim points to the donkeys. "The king sends more copper and tin aboard these beasts of burden so that the greatness of his temple shall know no bounds. Your toil shall fill it with treasures such as his people have never seen."

He pauses, seeming to wait for cheers, forgetting that almost of his audience are Phoenicians. Not King Solomon's people. Not Joakim's people. For that matter, not Jehovah's people.

"Are you Huram of Tyre?" Joakim asks, gesturing in Huram's direction. "Are you the man who will show me the king's treasures?"

I wonder how he made the correct guess. Do the rich and powerful smell better than the rest of us? I would surely hope so. Or is it just the wide girth of those with the means to eat more than just their daily bread?

"Yes, I am Huram." The smug look returns to his face. Surprising us all, he bows. "At the king's service with what talents I may possess."

What talents I may possess. Like Esau of old and his hunger for a bowl of porridge, I would forfeit my birthright, if I had one, for the chance to slap this arrogant man. Such is my hunger.

"Then you shall lead me to the storehouse where the

completed pieces have been collected," Joakim says. "I shall inspect them to see that the king will not be disappointed."

"He will not be disappointed," Huram says. "You may be certain of that. You know of my talents and I've brought with me the most renowned bronze-working artisans from the great city of Tyre. Our work shall please the king, of that I am sure."

The most renowned bronze-working artisans from the great city of Tyre. While the Phoenicians look on in pride, I try to recall who he might have omitted. Hmm. I wonder. Abimael's lips are pursed so tightly they are turning white. I want to spit on the ground. Elam himself looks on with heavy-lidded eyes, not seeming to care about the insult. Content, even when he has no right to be.

I now have another subject I'd like to slap.

———

THREE GUARDS STAND outside the storehouse, their spears sharp and their shields bearing the king's seal. Because of that seal, the treasures destined for the temple are safe within the storehouse; a man who violates that seal forfeits his life.

The guards move aside and Joakim and Huram step forward. Everyone else gathers around along the two walls closest to the entrance.

The larger pieces are arrayed on thick wood planking, protecting them from ground moisture; the smaller ones rest on solid wood tables. Smooth cloths cover each one, concealing them from view.

Huram strides to the nearest table and faces Joakim.

"These will decorate the temple's front pillars when they

are completed," Huram says. With a flourish, he yanks off the cloth.

Fifty brass pomegranates cover the table, the red-gold shimmering of the bronze making it look like gold itself.

Joakim draws in his breath sharply. He moves to within a hand's breadth to examine them more closely.

"What detail!" Joakim exclaims. "The fruit looks like it is about to burst open."

Huram steps to the next table. "These also will decorate the pillars."

He pulls aside the cloth to display four linked chains of bronze curling back on each other, each one extending over thirty paces long.

Joakim nods his approval.

Huram skips past the tables he once derisively referred to as "the Israelite section" and moves to a large form resting on the planking. He yanks off the cloth.

An immense bronze ox stares at the king's envoy, its black eyes lifelike, its great tail in the midst of swatting away invisible flies.

Joakim continues his praise.

Huram moves through the other major pieces, giving special attention to a lion with a most lifelike mane, until only two remain. He stands before a cloth covering a piece that rises to his chest. The room seems to hold its collective breath. Even I await the verdict.

Huram delicately removes the cloth, displaying a bronze water lily almost four feet tall, its petals and stem a work of art, one that I concede is far beyond my abilities or Elam's of Abimael's and will always be so.

Joakim's face flushes as if besotted by a beautiful woman. "It's magnificent!" He examines the fine detail, the way the stems bend in such a lifelike fashion. "King Solomon will be amazed."

Huram beams. He waits for Joakim to recover before they move on.

"And the final piece," Huram says, his voice shaking with excitement as he pulls aside the cloth. "The cherubim."

The work depicts five of them, each with wings unfurled and cheeks glowing with the bronze's red-gold shimmer. Their hands meet in the middle where in King Solomon's temple, they will hold a candle with their finely detailed fingers.

Joakim gasps. He cannot speak. A hand moves to his mouth.

"This work is extraordinary," he says finally. "The king..." He shakes his head. "Just extraordinary. Huram, you are a master. And your men are artisans of the highest order."

Joakim surveys the room. "Is everyone here?" he asks, then looks at Huram. "Except for the slaves, of course."

Huram counts us to be sure. He nods. "Yes."

"Tonight," Joakim says, "we shall have a feast of celebration for I will be bringing the king the greatest of reports. His temple will be a great wonder, the most splendid to be found." He spreads his hands wide. "Tonight we shall kill the fatted calf and drink the king's wine."

The room erupts in cheers. Elam pounds his hands together. Even grim Abimael allows himself a smile.

Joakim holds up his hand for silence.

"I am also authorized to grant each man a bonus of five shekels payable on the morrow." The cheering erupts even louder. He leans toward Huram and whispers something. Huram nods and smiles.

I wonder at the size of Huram's bonus, surely their topic of discussion, until Elam claps me on the shoulder.

"I told you they'd take care of us," he says.

"The Lord provides for his people," Abimael says.

"Now you can stop being so cynical," Elam says, that jovial face of his beaming even more broadly. "Tonight we shall drink of the king's wine, partake of the fatted calf, and roll the dice to separate the Phoenicians from their shekels."

Even as Abimael frowns, I feel my spirits soar.

Now *that* will be a fitting end to the evening.

———

ELAM AND I eat and drink until the night is late, as do all the men from Tyre, even the master himself, Huram, who partakes enough of the fatted calf to expand his girth in just the one meal. We sing merry songs that grow more bawdy by the hour, even joining in with the Phoenicians.

Only Abimael retires early, the merriment too much for his disposition, a feisty psalm about all he can handle.

Joakim drinks little, choosing instead to send his portions to Elam and me, which we gratefully accept. I've never known my friend to decline a skin of wine.

Elam and I take on the Phoenicians in some rolls of the dice, but sadly it is they who separate us from our shekels and not the other way around.

When we have lost all our money and drank all the wine, Elam and I stagger back to his father's tent, commiserating in our losses, certain the Phoenicians cheated but unsure how. We're drunk enough that we can barely say the words, much less figure out how we lost.

We enter the tent and collapse onto the ground, knowing the morning will come all too soon.

———

BUT IT ISN'T MORNING. The night is still dark and Abimael is shaking us both awake.

"Do you hear that?" he whispers urgently.

I rub my eyes. My stomach roils. From the other side of the tent, I hear Elam groan.

"Listen!" Abimael says.

I lift my head but hear nothing.

"They're just having fun," I say, my speech slurred.

"No, not that way. Over there." Abimael points toward the storehouse. "Come with me."

But I can't clear my head. I actually make it onto all fours but then topple over.

"You two!" Abimael says in disgust and then leaves.

An instant before I fall back asleep, I hear Elam snore.

———

"*WHERE IS ABIMAEL*?" a deep, angry voice bellows.

I lift my head off the ground and groan. The harsh words echo painfully in my head; bright sunlight pierces my eyes. Several paces away, Elam moans, sounding as bad as I feel.

I make out two of the largest Phoenicians, ugly and imposing, glaring at us from the mouth of the tent.

"Where is Abimael?" says the larger of the two. An old scar runs along his eyebrow.

I push myself up on one elbow. Everything spins until I close my eyes. I open them and try to focus on the spot where Abimael should be lying. He's not there.

The Phoenician with the scar turns toward the storehouse and yells, "It is the Israelites! It is Abimael!"

The two men drag us roughly to our feet and haul us

outside. I try to clear my mind even as my stomach roils. I vaguely recall Abimael waking us in the middle of the night and saying something about the storehouse. But what?

"Bring me the Israelites!" a voice bellows from over by the storehouse. Huram.

Elam and I stare at each other. Elam's eyes widen.

"I shall have their heads!" Huram continues.

As the two Phoenicians drag us toward the storehouse, others rush at us from every direction, quickly surrounding us, fury in their eyes. The one with the scar says, "They would steal the treasures from their own temple!" He spits on the ground before our feet.

Elam looks at me with alarm. After so many years of seeing that ruddy face without a care in the world, that look chills me. Far more than the spit of an ugly Phoenician.

"Where is my father?" Elam says, his voice filled with fear.

"Where indeed," the scarred Phoenician says.

The rest of the camp, save the slaves, is gathered at the storehouse. The three daytime guards stand before the entrance even though their watch is not yet due. Though day has broken, this is still the hour for the night watch.

As he sees us come nigh, Huram's face turns almost purple with rage. "What have you done with them?" Behind Huram, Joakim glares.

"Done with what?" I ask.

"My treasures," Huram says. "The two prize pieces. The cherubim and the water lilies. They are my greatest works. I must have them back!"

"The *king*," Joakim says with cold fire in his voice, "must have them back."

A pang of regret passes over Huram's face, and then he nods. "Yes, the *king* must have them back."

"We know not of what you speak," I say, knowing that no matter what the answer, it bodes ill for us.

"Where is my father?" Elam says.

"We have searched the entire camp," Joakim says coldly. "Every Phoenician and every slave is accounted for. Only Abimael is missing. The reason is clear. In the dead of night, he stole the treasures and fled." Joakim's eyes narrow. "After killing the king's three guards."

My jaw drops. To be accused by Huram or any of his men is a fearsome enough thing; we are but three amidst a den of vile Phoenicians. But for a fellow Israelite, a representative of the great King Solomon, to make the charge turns me cold.

"Do not pretend that you do not know," Joakim says.

"Why do you speak ill of my father?" Elam says. "He has never stolen so much as a shekel in his life. He is the most honest man I know."

"Then why is he, and he alone, missing?" Joakim asks.

I recall now Abimael asking us to join him, then leaving without us for the storehouse, but I can scarcely admit that. Those words would condemn him further still. I look to Elam, who stares helplessly back.

"The thief is missing," Huram thunders, "because he has fled with the cherubim and water lilies. Why else?" He points at us, as he has so often in the past, though then only to sneer. Now it means our lives. "The Israelites are not like us." He looks at Joakim, realizes that he, too, is an Israelite, and flushes. "The three of them share their own tent. They share their own counsel, eating and working together, apart from my men. The hold back no secrets from each other. These two know where Abimael is. They must. They will lead us to the treasures."

"Guards," Joakim says to the three guards. "Seize these two men."

The lead guard, a man with whom I shared a riddle but three days ago, and two others, one on each side, stand before Elam and me, their spears ready.

In a trembling voice, Elam asks, "What have you done with my father?"

I try to piece it together. Who could have stolen the cherubim and water lilies? Where are they now? What happened and when? And where is Abimael? What did he do after he left our tent? And why does Joakim suspect an Israelite over so many men of Tyre?

Some of the answers, one in particular, I fear I already know. My mind, lost in a fog just minutes ago but now clear as a bright summer day, races but not fast enough.

"I must depart to report to the king," Joakim says. "My men are preparing the animals now."

The Phoenicians begin to murmur, glancing angrily amongst themselves. The word "shekels" can clearly be heard. They care only of their own greed, not of the lives of Israelites. I wonder which of them has committed this treachery.

Joakim glares at them. "I will pay your shekels upon my return so long as the stolen treasures are found," he says. "Surely you do not expect the king to pay a bonus when the most prized treasures are missing."

The Phoenicians fall silent and stare at the ground as the King's carriage, drawn by the two white horses, arrives. The driver turns it around and waits. Over a hundred paces away, Joakim's two men are on their black horses leading away the beasts of burden. Two of the donkeys appear so lame I wonder if they'll survive the trip back to Jerusalem.

"Must you tell the king about the theft?" Huram asks. He

licks his lips. "A king's anger is a hard thing to suffer. Many treasures remain. Almost all of them, in fact. The great ox. The lion. The pomegranates and chain links for the pillars. We will find the thief Abimael. The treasures will come back to the storehouse."

"And if you fail?" Joakim asks. "If you never see the treasures again?"

Huram looks as though he's been told of the death of his firstborn. My hatred of the man almost distracts me into pleasure at his agony. "I will get them back," he says. "I *must* get them back." His jaw sets. "And if not, then we shall make others that are their equal. I swear it."

"And what of the death of the guards?"

Huram blinks. His obsession over his lost treasures has blinded him to the deaths of the three men. And almost certainly, I think, a fourth.

"The slaves will bury them," he says. "I will send word to their families."

"But the king must send replacements bearing his seal."

Huram's shoulders slump. "That is true."

"The king must be told of the guards," Joakim says. "But I will spare you the king's wrath over the lost treasures, so long as the next time I arrive, they have been replaced."

With sudden clarity, I see it all inside my head. What happened. What I must do.

I step forward, fury welling up within me.

"I can tell you where the treasures are," I say.

Joakim looks startled.

"Where are my cherubim and water lilies?" Huram says. "You know where Abimael has taken them?"

"I know not of Abimael, though I have my fears," I say. I clench my fists in rage.

"This man speaks in riddles," Joakim says. "Guard, take him away!"

I glare at Joakim, hating him more now than Huram and all his Phoenicians combined. "The bronze cherubim and water lilies ride aboard this man's donkeys," I say. "The two that are near to collapsing from the weight." I point to where Joakim's men are leading the beasts of burden away.

Joakim strikes me across the face. "How dare you insult me, envoy of the great King Solomon?"

I resist the urge to strike him back. He is the king's representative, though for but a few moments more if I am right.

"Prove me wrong," I say, knowing my life weighs in the balance, if it is not already forfeit. "Tell your men to return here."

"I'll not take orders from a prisoner!"

I turn to the guards. "This man killed your three comrades. Will you protect him now?"

"I'll listen to this no more," Joakim says, his voice quivering.

He goes to board the carriage, but Huram grabs his arm. "Did you steal my water lilies? The cherubim?"

The guard I shared the riddle with blocks Joakim's way. "If you killed my comrades, you broke the king's seal and will be condemned to death. We will go to your animals. If the treasures are not there, the prisoner dies. But if the prisoner is right--"

"Stop this madness!" Joakim says, but the guards continue to block his way.

In little time, we overtake Joakim's men. Their horses could outrace us, but the heavily burdened donkeys cannot.

The lead guard moves close to the first beast. It arrived to the foundry with a large, coarse sack strapped atop its back, the sack loaded with copper or tin for smelting. Now, the sack remains filled to overflowing, as does the one other. Two donkeys are carrying heavy sacks; the others, nothing.

I hold my breath as the guard slashes the sack. At first, only sand pours out, and I feel my own life departing with it. But then the wondrous red-gold shimmer of bronze appears.

Huram stumbles over to protect the piece from falling. He guides it out safely, like a midwife with a newborn, and holds the brass cherubim in his trembling hands.

"When Joakim saw the cherubim and the lilies," I say, "he had to possess them. He could not share them with all the people of Israel. Such was his greed. They had to be his own.

"He offered shekels he would never have to pay so that we would celebrate, then got us drunk so that only the three guards would stand between him and the treasures, guards who would naturally show deference to the king's envoy and be easily slain with the help of his two men."

I look about. Every eye is either on me or is shifting to Joakim with a look of disbelief.

"One more man, however, stood between him and the treasures," I say. "Abimael, the one man who did not partake beyond what thirst required of the king's wine. And when he left his tent for the storehouse and discovered Joakim's treachery, he paid for it with his life."

All eyes now are on Joakim, who stands silent and unwavering, lips pursed.

"Where did you bury him?" Elam asks, tears streaming down his dirt-streaked face.

Joakim's men leap aboard their horses and try to race off, but the Phoenicians yank them down and throw them to the ground. Joakim stares straight ahead.

I look to Huram, whose guilt I had so desired but been

denied. "Why would Joakim conceal the theft from the king if not to insure the safety of the treasures in his own hands? Did you think he would risk his life as a favor to you?" I spare the vain man no more than I've spared Joakim. "Not every man loves you, Huram, as much as you love yourself."

Huram winces. After a time, he points to the sack strapped to the other donkey. Once again, the guard uses his spear and cuts open the sack. Sand pours out until the bronze water lily slowly appears.

It is broken in two, its delicate stem severed.

A wail escapes from Huram's lips. He grabs the nearest guard's spear. I guess that the guard knows what is about to happen but has allowed the weapon to slip through his hands.

Huram leans back and plunges the spear into Joakim's chest.

Joakim gasps. His eyes grow pleasurably wide. He drops to his knees, grasping at the spear even as the ground about him turns dark red.

Death comes fast.

But not with nearly enough pain.

NEAT FREAK

INTRODUCTION TO "NEAT FREAK"

Neat Freak" is the first of three very short stories. At 1000 words, it's on, or over, the boundary of flash fiction. Either way, it's a fun return to modern times. It's the first, but not the last, you'll see of Boston's subway system, known as the T (short for MBTA, which is short for Massachusetts Bay Transportation Authority).

Can you hear the screech of the rails? Can you smell the musty air and the odor of stale sweat?

Hold on tight. It could be a rough ride.

NEAT FREAK

Kellie O'Reilly thought nothing of the short, baby-faced man in the business suit who climbed onto the Blue Line subway car behind her. But that was understandable. He hadn't pointed a gun at her yet.

Plenty of people boarded with them at the Government Center stop headed north so she barely noticed him, no more than she noticed the pervasive grime, the smells of stale sweat and cheap perfume, and the screeching of other cars coming in and out of the station. A meticulously neat person, Kellie couldn't completely ignore the dirty floor and surfaces—were all subways this filthy?—and the empty Lay's potato chip bag on the floor gnawed at her like sewer rat, but the irksome sights and smells and sounds had faded further into the background each time she rode the T.

As she took her seat, her mind was on the project due for next week's Analysis of Algorithms class. Professor Harris had assigned it three weeks ago but had only clarified key concepts in tonight's lecture. Terrified that this one project might ruin her perfect 4.0 GPA, Kellie scribbled ideas into her notebook. She thought only about how to restructure the code and not at all about the dwindling number of passengers nor the baby-faced man in the business suit on the opposite side of the car.

"I like redheaded Irish girls," the baby-faced man said softly, no longer on the other side of the car but looming over her, smiling.

Kellie looked up at him, saw the cold steel glint in his eyes, and then looked wildly about, noticing only then that the car was empty except for the two of them and an elderly couple a good fifty feet away.

She froze, suddenly aware of everything about her: the rocking of the subway car, the pungent smell of the man's cologne, and the empty potato chip bag rocking on the dirty black-and-white tiled floor.

"You're Irish, I can tell," Baby Face said. "An Irish redhead. Just my type. We should have a few drinks together. You drink, don't you? Of course you do."

"Please leave me alone," Kellie said, her voice shaking.

Baby Face smiled. "I don't think so." He slid a hand inside his right suit pocket and wiggled it. The outline of a gun pointing at her formed in the pocket.

Kellie's eyes widened.

"Get off with me at the next stop," Baby Face said. "Nice and quiet, if you know what's good for you."

Kellie's chest tightened. Icy tentacles of fear gripped her. She couldn't move, couldn't breathe.

Baby Face wagged the gun. "*Comprende?*"

A voice broke in, his words crackling over the loudspeaker, and for the briefest instant Kellie thought she'd been rescued. Then the words registered. "Next stop, Revere Beach." And again. "Next stop, Revere Beach."

Kellie's heart hammered. A statistic, that's what she was

going to become. In her mind's eye she saw her lifeless body, tossed in a dumpster with the rotting garbage and rats as large as cats. Gnawing at her after Baby Face had finished his business.

She shuddered, wanting to scream but unable to so much as open her mouth.

"*Comprende*?" Baby Face said again, his voice hard and cold. The smile had left his face, replaced by an angry glare.

Kellie stared at him, unable to answer, unable to even nod. Stiff as a corpse. A corpse in a dumpster.

A scream welled up within her but couldn't escape.

Baby Face stepped closer. "Don't even think about it."

Kellie looked into his eyes and felt her head swim.

The subway car slowed.

The voice again crackled over the loudspeakers. "Entering the Revere Beach station. Revere Beach."

The old couple prepared to leave. The lights momentarily flickered.

"Get up," Baby Face said and waggled the gun, icy steel in his voice. "Now."

Kellie looked all about. At the map of all the subway stops. At the advertisements. At the dirty floor and the empty potato chip bag.

That wasn't empty.

A large black cockroach crawled out of it. Not just large. Huge. Almost the size of Kellie's thumb.

Revulsion flooded over her.

The cockroach crept toward her.

The subway car stopped and Baby Face said something, but Kellie only saw the cockroach.

Moving closer.

Toward her.

Kellie screamed, loud and long.

On some distant subconscious level she sensed Baby Face bolting for the door, but her eyes never left the roach.

Her scream continued as the doors closed, separating her forever from Baby Face but closing her in with the filthy thing.

Waddling ever closer.

Her skin crawled.

She'd have to kill it. She fought back a gagging sensation.

Closing her eyes, she lifted her foot to stomp on it.

The cockroach stopped.

Something bubbled up from deep within Kellie.

An Irish redhead. Just my type.

She glanced up and saw that Baby Face was gone. She'd known that he was gone on some level but at the same time hadn't really *known* that he was gone.

The subway car rocked back and forth as it sped onward to the last stop, her stop.

Without Baby Face and his gun.

An Irish redhead. Just my type.

Kellie stared at the cockroach and then at her own foot, still raised to stomp out the filthy thing.

She looked out the window at the landscape rushing by.

And thought of Baby Face in his nicely pressed suit with the gun in its right pocket.

Slowly Kellie lowered her foot to the floor. Nowhere near the roach. There would be no disgusting crunch of its shell beneath her foot, no smear of its guts when she lifted her foot.

Filled with both revulsion and a strange sense of gratitude, Kellie moved around the cockroach, giving it a wide berth, to the furthest seat she could find.

They'd both dodged a bullet.

THE KIDS KEEP COMING

INTRODUCTION TO "THE KIDS KEEP COMING"

My first attempt at writing this introduction resulted in a long, dreary discussion of race in America today. I hated it, and you would have, too. So I chucked it.

"The Kids Keep Coming" is going to have to speak for itself.

I wrote it in response to a call for stories about taverns. I wrote it in response to events on the news. That intersection produced "The Kids Keep Coming."

The story appeared in *Fiction River: Tavern Tales*. The following year, it was a Best Short Story finalist for the Derringer Award, an honor bestowed by the Short Mystery Fiction Society.

It's a haunting tale that I hope lingers long after you read it.

THE KIDS KEEP COMING

THEY'RE ALL UNDERAGE, of course. It's a requirement. So the hardest drink I can serve here at the *Sweet Chariot* is a lemonade or pop.

Outside, the rotted wooden sign hangs at an angle, held in place by a single remaining, rusted nail, tacked onto the weathered clapboards beside the door frame. The sign's white paint blistered and peeled long ago so the black lettering is hard to make out in the thick, wet fog that never lifts. But those who need to read it can make out its words.

COLOREDS ONLY

OVER 18 NOT WELCOME

NO EXCEPTIONS

They step inside the door looking confused and scared, even the older teenagers. They look at me with distrust or maybe anger, and who can blame them? Some step back outside to look again at the sign before returning to look at me, their skins ranging from lightest brown to darkest black but mine undeniably white.

I'm an old man, dressed in a fraying, gray, button-down shirt and dark pants, with liver spots on hands I can barely hold steady. Some days the shakes are so bad it's all I can do to hand over a bottle of Coke without sloshing the whole damned thing all across the stained, dark wood counter top.

"What'll ya have?" I ask a youngster who's just walked in the front door. He's maybe fifteen, rail thin but close to six feet tall, skin dark as coal, wearing a gold-and-purple LA Lakers jersey and cut jeans. A purple Lakers cap, facing backwards, covers most of his close-cropped hair. His eyes are haunted, as is the case for almost all who enter here, but they also flash with anger. In his wake walks a younger boy, certainly his brother based on the strong resemblance, maybe twelve or thirteen. He wears cut jeans as well, but with only a plain, white T-shirt.

"I got Coke, Diet Coke, Dr. Pepper, Mountain Dew, and lemonade," I say.

The younger one looks like he's ready to respond, but the older one shakes his head. "Don't need nothing you got."

Maybe it's the damned sign outside. It was here when I arrived, just part of the empty building. I don't know who put it there. Over the years, I've considered putting up a new one, getting rid of the word COLOREDS. Change it to NEGROES, then BLACKS, and now AFRICAN AMERI-CANS. But I've never found a piece of wood, paint, nails or a hammer. Those things just aren't around.

It doesn't seem to matter. The kids find their way here no matter what. Probably would walk inside even if I put up a stop sign, or a skull-and-crossbones. Doesn't matter, eventu-ally the kids get comfortable enough to tell their stories while they sip on a nice cold pop. Or soda, as some of them call it, though back home in Detroit, it was pop and will forever remain that for me.

"It's free," I say to the two boys.

"And you white," the older one says.

I nod and grab a glass from a tray of them sitting on a shelf a foot below the bar top. I begin to polish the glasses, one by one. The three of us are alone, and the boys take in their surroundings. Quivering dark walls, barely thirty feet to both sides of us, shimmer like air atop asphalt on a hot Detroit summer day. There was a time, until about fifty or sixty years ago, this place was damned near as wide as a football field is long, its walls bulging at the seams, stretching wider and wider. But over the years the walls have contracted, like an organism finding less and less to feed on, closing in on itself till now it feels tiny.

It's a trickle of kids coming in compared to the old days. But still a steady trickle.

A damned steady trickle.

"I'll take a lemonade," the younger one says, and takes a seat on one of the seven stools, just to my right of center. He has to almost jump on top of it and wiggle himself into place, ignoring the glare of his older brother. "I'm Marcus and I'm twelve. This is my brother, Jamaal. He's fifteen."

"Don't talk to him," Jamaal says, though he sits on the middle stool as I busy myself pouring freshly squeezed lemonade into the glass I've just polished. "Specially about me. Don't never talk about me. But you, too. Ain't you got no sense?"

Marcus looks downcast at the bar, eyes filled with sorrow. With my hands shaking so bad the lemonade is splashing over the edge and onto my hand and the bar top, I set the glass in front of Marcus, on a black coaster with a red center that says Coca-Cola. I grab a plain white towel off the lower shelf and wipe away the spill and dry my hands, noting that the towel is still damp from the last time and next time I need it, it'll probably be soon enough so it'll still be damp. Considering all the stains on the bar top, coasters may seem a bit silly, but to my mind they give this place the tiniest air of class. I think that's something these kids deserve.

"Ain't you got no TV?" Jamaal asks.

I think of pointing out that when I first came here in '59, most folks alive in the US had a TV, but it was black and white. No one had color TVs in those days because there wasn't no color TV programs. But I know that neither of these kids want to hear about the old days, life before color TVs, iPhones, and videogames, which I hear them talk about but still can't quite figure out what they mean. So I keep my message short.

"I'm your only entertainment," I say.

Jamaal shakes his head. "Shiiiit." He pulls from his jeans pocket what serves as a passport of sorts in these parts. It has a grainy, stiff exterior and an interior that pops open exposing his photo as he tosses it on the bar. "Marcus, give yours to the old guy and let's get out of here."

Marcus fishes his out of his pocket, opens it to his photo, and places it beside his brother's. He takes a long drink of the lemonade.

"Doesn't work that way," I say.

"I knew it," Jamaal says with disgust.

"You have to tell me your story," I say. "How you came to be here. Then I stamp your book."

"We walked through the fog," Jamaal says. "Came to this place. Stepped inside. Now stamp our damned books and let us get the hell out of here."

"No, the *real* story," I say. "That's what you did after the real story happened. What happened so you had to come here?"

"That how you get your rocks off, old man? You some kind of perv? Must be. Your little, wrinkled white dick gets stiff hearing about black boys dying. You gotta hear every last detail?"

It takes a long time before I answer. "It breaks my heart every time."

"I bet!"

Silence hangs heavy in the air. It stretches out longer and longer and as it does I almost feel the glimmering dark walls contract ever so slightly, closing in on us the barest fraction of an inch.

"Maybe we should—" Marcus says tentatively.

"Shut up!" Jamaal says.

After a time, I say, "Stay here as long as you want. There's no hurry." I wait, then say, "But I can't stamp your book until you tell me your story."

"Says who?"

"It's the rule," I say. "And you can't move on to whatever comes next unless I stamp your book."

"What comes next?" Marcus asks, and for once Jamaal doesn't cut him off or tell him to shut up. Jamaal wants to know that answer as much as Marcus does.

Unfortunately, as much as I do, too.

"I don't know," I say. "This is where I've been ever since I crossed over. I don't know what's outside that door other than the fog and the exterior of this building."

"The Man screws us from the day we born," Jamaal says, turning to Marcus. "And The Man screws us till the day we die. Then He start screwing us again all over. The Man makes all the rules, and we supposed to just say, 'yessir,' Whitey here don't know shit, but we got to tell him our stories, else we can't move on. We stuck here with this sorry ass geezer, like he's got a gun to our heads. Like he be a cop gonna do a choke hold and make us gasp for breath we don't do what he say."

Jamaal turns to me. "Before we tell you anything about us, you gonna tell us *everything* about you. How you like that, whitebread?"

"Fair enough."

Jamaal reacts with a start. He was all set to continue arguing, but I've stolen his thunder.

I draw air through my nostrils noisily and begin. I've told the story so many, many times before.

"I was a cop," I begin, and Jamaal explodes out of his seat.

"*Whaaat?*"

"In fact, that's why I'm here," I say. "You might say I'm serving a sentence."

———

I SHOT A KID. A black kid. Fourteen years old. And yet that isn't why I'm here.

It was 1955, and I was a rookie cop. Green as I could be. I'd say I was just out of the academy, but back then there were no police academies. I got paired with an Irish cop named Patrick O'Sullivan, originally from Boston. Everyone called him Sully. I wouldn't have been surprised if his paycheck was just made out to Sully. I didn't wonder, at the time, why he'd ever left his hometown for Detroit. It was only later that I'd consider that perhaps he'd been asked to leave.

One day, my second week on the job, we got a call to go into the projects. Gang problems. Sully called the projects Negro Town, although Negro wasn't really the word he used, if you know what I mean.

We went in, flying up the stairwell with its single dangling lightbulb, wooden steps half rotted out, and an eye-watering stench of urine you figured would stick with you for days. Next thing we knew, the lights went out and this kid came out of his apartment, holding a revolver pointed straight at Sully. I couldn't even see the kid, just a dark figure in the doorway.

He fired a split second after Sully ducked.

I had no choice.

I had to shoot. Had to take him down.

And as the kid went down, a beam of light suddenly turned on inside the apartment, illuminated his face, a face with a jagged, four-inch scar directly underneath the right eye.

And I saw the look of shock.

He hadn't known we were police. We hadn't had the chance to announce ourselves. He thought it was a rival gang come to take him down. We weren't the rival gang's hit squad. We just did their work for them.

I did their work for them. I had no choice, and he didn't have a chance.

That kid's shock-filled face filled my nightmares for over a year. His appearances only became less frequent because he had competition. You see, that kid isn't why I'm where I am today. I was put in a no-win situation. I had no choice. Kill or be killed. In fact, Sully screamed at me for days that if I didn't do a better job of defending him next time, he'd shoot me himself.

He used that against me.

A week later, he shot a seventeen-year-old black kid in the back who was running away from him, and then expected me to cover for him.

"What are you looking at?" Sully said. "Don't you dare

get righteous on me. Your gutlessness almost got me killed a week ago. Don't you forget who your brother is. Your brother in blue."

He stood over the dead kid. "The world's better off without this piece of shit."

And so I backed him up. Signed off on the bullshit story he made up. Perjured myself for my partner, my brother in blue.

And the next time. And the time after that. I agreed to all the lies, the fabricated evidence. I looked the other way when Sully got out a throw down gun and placed it in the thin, soft brown hands of another goddamned kid.

Inevitably, a couple of them were white. Eventually an Asian or two. Sully didn't totally discriminate. But almost every last one of them was black.

When I finally couldn't take it anymore—the last time it was a sweet-looking, eleven-year-old girl who they said sang like Mahalia Jackson in her church choir, a little eleven-year-old girl for Chrissakes—I didn't rat him out to Internal Affairs. I didn't stop him.

I just asked for a new partner. Made up some story as bullshit as Sully's explanations for his growing death toll. And I stepped aside.

Didn't change a thing. Didn't stop him. I just made it easier on my conscience because it wasn't happening right in front of my eyes anymore. I could pretend it wasn't happening anymore. With Sully and the others in the department who were almost as bad.

Hey, sometimes like with the kid with a jagged scar there's nothing a cop can do. It's a tough, dangerous job. Lots of funerals on the side of the blue.

But the numbers with Sully didn't lie.

I *knew*, goddamit. I *knew*.

And I said nothing. I did nothing to stop him.

That's why I'm here. I've been sentenced to spend an eternity here, watching boys like you walk in, your lives cut cruelly short.

And I have to listen.

Because I knew and said nothing. I fucking knew.

———

WHEN I FINISH, Jamaal snorts. "Poor baby." And then, "You deserve to suffer."

"When did you die?" Marcus asks.

"I stayed on the force for five years," I say. "Ate my gun when I was twenty-nine."

"Wish you had pictures," Jamaal says.

I can't blame him.

A frown forms on Marcus's brow. "Twenty nine?"

I nod.

"But...if Jamaal still looks like he's fifteen and I still look like I'm twelve," Marcus says, cocking his head to the side. "How come you don't look like you're twenty-nine? No offense but—"

"You look like you just crawled out of a freaking grave," Jamaal says.

I nod. Another question I've heard so many times before. "You're as old as you feel."

Marcus nods thoughtfully.

When the time is right, they tell me their story. As are all the stories I hear, it involves police killing a young black boy or girl. In this case, their one story involves two boys, for they died together. I can only imagine how their parents themselves died inside that day.

Jamaal and Marcus were playing together in the park

with toy guns. They rarely played together, their age difference of fifteen and twelve amounting to a Grand Canyon most of the time.

Tragically, though, not this day.

It was late on a Saturday, but still before dusk. Plenty of sunlight to see. Police shot Jamaal first, though he hadn't pointed the toy gun in their direction. A single shot in the chest.

And after Marcus whirled in the direction of the gunfire, his toy gun was pointed at them. Six bullets between the two cops ripped apart his thin, twelve-year-old chest.

————

"WHY YOU?" MARCUS asks. "Why are you here instead of Sully?"

I shrug. It's a question I've asked myself many, many times, and the same answer keeps coming back. "Because I'm guilty."

"But Sully was guilty of even more," Marcus says.

"Maybe Sully and the other ones like him, the ones with no conscience, no hope of redemption, went straight to Hell." I shrug. "Although I'm not sure I really believe in Hell anymore. Maybe Hell isn't eternal fiery brimstone. It's listening to you kids and have my heart ripped open time after time. There aren't as many of you as in the old days, but sometimes I don't think I can take anymore."

Jamaal snorts. "You the victim. How white of you. You shoot a brother dead and let a psychopath kill who knows how many more and we're supposed to feel bad for you? Are you shitting me? *You're* the victim?"

"I'm no victim," I say. I can see that he feels no sympathy

for my situation and I can't blame him. In a way, I feel no sympathy for myself either.

"You want me to kill you, put you out of your misery?" Jamaal asks. "Do it in a heartbeat."

It's a thought. But it's the easy way out.

I shake my head. "I did the crime. I'll do the time."

"You'll be here forever?" Marcus asks.

I remain silent for a long time even though it's a question I've heard many times before. I sigh. "I guess I stay here until finally, some day, no more of you kids walk through that door. Maybe the day comes when I can just close up shop. Lock the doors and throw away the keys. Then I'll be able to move on myself. To whatever comes next.

"Ain't never gonna stop," Jamaal says, and slides his passport to me.

I nod and pull out the knife with a razor-sharp, six-inch blade and well-worn grip from beneath the counter. I unbutton my work shirt, exposing the old scars that populate my wrinkled skin. I slice a shallow vertical cut down my chest between the two rib cages.

The blood trickles onto my writing finger. I press it firmly onto the passport, giving a good print so it's unmistakable that it's mine.

I repeat the process for Marcus.

"You two are all set," I say. "When you're ready, step outside the door and you'll find your way to whatever comes next. I wish you the best."

Jamaal spins and leaves. Marcus lingers. "I hope someday you can join us."

But I know, deep in my heart, that this place isn't ever shutting its doors. I ain't never moving on. It's not like the old days when I had to slit my wrists to stamp all the books for those kids. But there's still a trickle.

A steady damned trickle.
The kids just keep coming.

HOLD UP

INTRODUCTION TO "HOLD UP"

Here's another piece of flash fiction. If I say too much, the introduction will be longer than the story itself. So I'll just point out that "The Kids Keep Coming," which you just finished, had its real-world setting in Detroit. We'll stay in the Motor City (albeit with a trip across the border) for just a few hundred more words.

HOLD UP

When Jim Cassidy first started driving a cab in Detroit, he'd hated two things above all others: crossing the Ambassador bridge into Canada and dealing with drunks, especially rich ones. In recent years, though, he'd grown to appreciate the former and tolerate the latter.

After all, he had bills to pay. Lots of bills.

So as midnight beckoned, Jim returned to Caesars Casino on the Canadian side, and picked up the same rich drunk he'd dropped off a few hours earlier. A guy who'd tipped handsomely, more than enough to be worth Jim's trouble.

"The Marriott, my man," the rich drunk said. He slurred his words almost to the point of indecipherability, but it hardly mattered since Jim remembered where he'd picked the guy up in the first place. "The Dee-troit Marriott." The drunk whistled, spewing richly alcoholic fumes and a bit of spittle through the opening in the cloudy protective shield between the front and rear seats. "Seventy fucking floors, can you believe it?"

Jim nodded. He'd lived in Detroit all his life, all thirty-four years. He didn't need to be told how many floors the Marriott had or where the Red Wings and Pistons played or how Comerica Park stood right next to Ford Field and money rained down from heaven on those days when there were events going on at both. You could sit there in traffic with your passengers and the meter just ran and ran.

The rich drunk belched loudly as they approached customs, filling the air with his alcoholic fumes. They waited in a line just three cars deep and in no time the border guard was waving them up.

Jim pulled alongside the booth. He was in luck. It was Frankie, a wiry, fiftyish man with bushy gray hair. He and Frankie had gotten to know each other very well in recent years.

They both had bills to pay. Lots of bills to pay.

Jim met Frankie's eyes and rolled down the back window. Frankie took the drunk's passport and peered inside. "Why were you in Canada?"

The drunk belched again. "I was at the casino. Caesar's." His tone implied, *You got a problem with that?*

"What did you do at the casino?" Frankie asked.

"I was with my girlfriend," the drunk said, the belligerent tone now unmistakable. "Why?"

Jim sank back in his seat and relaxed. It was a done deal.

"What did you do with your girlfriend?" Frankie asked.

"*What?*" the drunk asked, incredulous.

"What did you do with your girlfriend?"

"None of your damned business," the drunk said. "What are you, some kind of a pervert?"

Jim almost broke into laughter. This was like taking candy from babies.

Frankie stepped back, then turned to Jim. He pointed to

another booth off to the side and up ahead. "Please drive over there, sir. We're going to have to proceed with a secondary screening."

The rich drunk began to spew obscenities, but Jim complied.

He grinned inwardly. The meter was still running; both he and Frankie had bills to pay.

CITY OF SIN STRANGLER

INTRODUCTION TO "CITY OF SIN STRANGLER"

And so we return to my beloved city of Lynn. I use the word beloved in an admittedly hypocritical manner. The relationship is more love-hate than beloved.

I can't accept the city's crime and violence. However, I do believe its reputation is far worse than the reality. If not for the unfortunate rhyme—"Lynn, Lynn, City of Sin, never come out, the way you went in"—the rep might not be half as bad as it is. Small wonder the city tried unsuccessfully to rename and rebrand itself as Ocean Park more than twenty years ago.

I love the way the city has fought back even as it has lost much of its industrial base. It has tried to revitalize its downtown, and I especially love the artists who have converted drab brick walls into gorgeous murals.

There may still be plenty of sinning in the City of Sin, but there's heart there, too.

So when I got the call for an anthology based on unlikely heroines, I placed my heroine in my City of Sin and gave her a heart, albeit a broken one, as huge in its own way as the city's. The editor didn't quite think "City of Sin Strangler" fit her anthology perfectly, but it got picked up by another volume of *Fiction River*, so I was delighted anyway.

I *love* this story. I think it's one of my best. And from the bottom of my heart, I love Rita, its unlikely heroine.

CITY OF SIN STRANGLER

The talk all around the city was the death of another prostitute. It was the second in three weeks, both by strangulation, both dumped near the entrance to the train station that took people from this gray, gritty city that smelled of smoke and car exhaust into Boston and back. The talk was nowhere near as overwhelming as it got about the Patriots or the Red Sox when they were in the playoffs—that was the important stuff—but there was talk.

Prostitutes were nothing new, of course, not worthy of mention other than the recurring references in the *Daily Item*'s Police Log, descriptions that had the feel of having been cut-and-pasted from all their predecessors with only a change in name and address. This city was, after all, known as "Lynn, Lynn, City of Sin (never come out, the way you went in)." Prostitutes were to Lynn what the Red Sox was to Boston.

Murder, on the other hand, was quite another thing. Lynn was bad, but it wasn't *that* bad. Murder was the exception, typically involving the drug deals that also littered the

Item's Police Log, usually only a handful every year, not the rule. Murders got people talking: waiting in line for coffee at Dunkin' Donuts; ordering a roast beef sandwich with mayo and cheese at Bill & Bob's; getting their vitals and medical history checked by Nora O'Sullivan before Dr. Frede, their urologist, arrived for the exam.

Nora heard it all. The attitude seemed to be that fortunately it was just whores walking the streets, selling their souls for their next high. Not good, honest people like them. Not people who counted.

They didn't say it in so many words. They used inference and euphemisms. But the message remained the same.

Not us. Just whores.

"We're better off without that scum," Charlie McGinty said in the most outspoken commentary so far, as Nora entered his vitals on her tablet. McGinty, now eighty-six, had visibly new dentures, thick-lensed glasses, and his white hair parted neatly on the side. He'd been coming to this office for forty-three years, slightly longer than Nora had been alive, and felt that he'd long since earned the privilege of stating his view on all matters that concerned him. "That's what I say. Good riddance to 'em all. If the killer gets a third one, I'll toss him a hat for the hat trick."

Nora, barely five feet tall and stocky with straight black hair cut short, felt the already small exam room close in on her. The all-white walls, bereft of any decoration save a near-life-sized chart showing the urologic internals of a male on the right and a female on the left, inched closer. The examining table on which McGinty was perched seemed to creep closer. Nora could smell his stale sweat, the cigarette smoke in his short-sleeved, white button-down shirt and his smoker's breath.

She just wanted to get away from this man. But she

needed this job, needed it in the worst way, and she knew the walls weren't really closing in. It was just those words, that attitude. She'd been hearing it all day, and from people who should know better. So she wouldn't totally rip into him. But she had to say something.

"For some mother or father," Nora said, looking Charlie McGinty right in the eye, "that dead girl is still their baby."

Charlie McGinty's head snapped back ever so slightly, as if she'd slapped him. He blinked, surprise covering his face, as if he'd been saying the same thing all day and only now had been contradicted even in the slightest.

"Well," he said. "There is that. God have mercy on them." He nodded thoughtfully, scratched the hint of white whisker stubble on his chin, and added, "Though if they'd-a brought her up right, took her to Mass every Sunday and didn't spare the rod, I bet she'd-a turned out better." He nodded in satisfaction and looked to Nora, apparently expecting a nod of agreement back.

Nora felt like volunteering to give Charlie McGinty his prostate exam herself, only with her whole damned fist, but just smiled weakly and told him the doctor would be in shortly.

As she shut the door softly behind her, her anger turned to tears. She ducked inside another exam room, still empty, before anyone could see. Only Dr. Frede himself knew, and she was damned if any of the others were going to find out.

There, but for the grace of God, go I, she thought. Not herself, of course. But Shannon, her twenty-one-year-old daughter, serving time now in MCI Framingham for a laundry list of offenses consisting primarily of drugs, prostitution, drugs, theft, and drugs. Not to mention skipping bail after Nora had scraped together every last cent of it, borrowing a good chunk, in fact, with no idea of how she'd pay it back.

Shannon. Every bit without value, in the eyes of most, as those two dead girls.

After Shannon skipped bail, Nora had sworn she was done with that girl. Finished. Kaput. But how did Nora spend a part of every weekend? Driving out to Framingham to see her daughter. What else could she do? She was Shannon's mother.

And when Shannon said, "Ma, I'm so sorry," Nora bought it. Knew it was genuine and from the heart, from one broken heart to another. Nora bought it even though she knew her girl—who had once had all the same dreams and ambitions as those who now verbally spat on her from their mighty, high horses—would almost certainly destroy herself again as soon as she got out. The hooks were in too deep. She'd stay clean for a while, but then her always-tenuous grip would slip, and she'd be back in the life.

Nora hoped to God that wasn't true, and had spent hours upon hours on her knees begging for another ending, but after a while, you just got so beaten down, it was hard to believe anymore.

Nora loved her daughter with all her heart. But Nora was so totally beaten down, she couldn't believe.

Wanted to. But couldn't.

———

NORA LUGGED the two bags of groceries up the winding, creaking, wooden steps to her third-floor apartment, wearily wondering how much new brakes would cost on the rusted-out, seventeen-year-old Hyundai she'd just left behind. The bucket of bolts had over 220,000 miles on it with tires so bald they'd never pass inspection this fall, much less be anything less than a death trap when snow hit in December. The engine went through oil so fast Nora had to top it off every week, and now the brakes were starting to grind. If it wasn't just the pads but the rotors, too, she didn't know how she'd pay for it.

They'd never been rich, but had managed to make ends meet and then a little some, their little family of four, until Mark left, deciding he'd met "the love of his life," talking as if sixteen years of marriage to Nora had been a goddamned prison sentence and Cindie, her younger, *far* more curvaceous replacement, made him feel alive again. Since the divorce almost six years ago, he'd complained almost nonstop about how he was always broke because of having to send Nora his hard-earned money, but the fact was they both were broke.

Of course, it didn't help that Josh, her fifteen-year-old son, was growing like a weed, almost six feet tall now, towering over her, always needing new clothes, new shoes and sneakers, new everything. And he had the metabolism of a furnace, able to eat three times what she ate and remain rail thin while no matter how she tried, Nora couldn't get rid of the pounds that had apparently made her so unattractive to Mark that he had to look elsewhere.

Josh, like all teenagers, burned through her money. But Nora begrudged him nothing. He was her pride and joy. All she had left, if truth be told. Almost straight A's, and never gave her even a hint of trouble. Made his bed every day. Kept his room clean. Helped out with chores without being asked, sometimes even making dinner.

"Yes, Mom."

"Sure."

"Okay, not a problem."

Those were his responses to almost any request. Nora could never say so out loud, but he was everything that Shannon was not. Sometimes she wondered how the two could come from the same genetic material and the same environment, yet turn out so different. If Josh ever got into trouble with drugs and turned out like Shannon, it would break her heart. The very thought chilled her to the marrow. It wasn't too late for that to happen. In fact, fifteen years old was pretty close to the bull's-eye. Dear God, please don't let him turn out like Shannon.

Nora shuddered, put the two grocery bags on the dark wooden stand by the door, and fished her keys out of her purse. She unlocked the door to the apartment, carried the bags inside, toed the door shut and walked through the front room, past Josh's closed bedroom door, and into the kitchen.

"How about cheeseburgers for dinner?" she called out. Most nights, she tried to be a bit healthier than that, but tonight she was just too damned tired.

"Sure," Josh yelled back.

Nora smiled and felt just a little less weary. "How many?"

"Three? Is that okay?"

And that was the thing of it. Josh didn't *want* to be expensive. He *asked* if three cheeseburgers was okay, *asked* if something other than the absolute cheapest jeans on the market would be okay, never demanded or grew sullen if the answer was no.

Minutes later as the cheeseburgers sizzled on the grill and Nora washed the lettuce and tomatoes in the sink, Josh appeared in the kitchen, wearing a black T-shirt, jeans, and white socks with no sneakers. Towering over her, he gave her a one-armed hug.

Nora stiffened and her eyes grew wide.

"What's that smell?" she demanded.

"I farted?" he said with a grin.

"Seriously!"

"You farted?"

"*What's that smell on your clothes*?" Nora yelled, her heart hammering in her chest like a drum. "Don't tell me, don't tell me, don't tell me."

Josh lifted the front of his T-shirt with his thumb and forefinger and took a whiff.

"Mom, a couple of guys on the bus were smoking weed. Not me. You need to chill out." He rested a hand on her shaking shoulder, bent over and kissed her on the top of the head.

"*Do you swear it*?"

"I told you, it wasn't me."

"Because if you turn out like—"

Nora stopped, but the words had come out and now that they were out there, they couldn't be recalled.

Now it was Josh who was angry. "How can you even *say* that?"

"I just—"

"I hate her! I hate what she's done to you!"

"I'm fine," Nora said, shaking her head. "Really, I'm fine. I was just scared that—"

"Do you *really* think I'm so stupid that after how she turned out I'd mess with that *shit*?" He stopped as both their eyes widened at his unexpected use of *that* word. "Give me a little more credit than that."

"Okay, okay. You're right!"

"Don't *ever* compare me to her!" he yelled.

And with that, Josh stormed out of the kitchen and into his bedroom, slamming the door behind him. It was perhaps, Nora thought guiltily, the only time he'd *ever* shown anger toward her.

————

THE BRAKES NEEDED new pads *and* new rotors. The landlord announced another rent increase effective the month after next, then took umbrage that his advance warning wasn't sufficiently appreciated. And a third prostitute was strangled and left on a downtown sidewalk, this time outside an optometrist's office.

The talk all around the city, once muted because the death was, after all, only a whore, became almost deafening, almost on par with the Red Sox in the World Series and the Patriots in the Super Bowl. There were headlines in the *Daily Item*, and press conferences by the Police Commissioner. As with the two previous victims, there was no sign of sexual assault, and the strangulation was achieved by use of a rope. Everyone had a theory—Jack the Ripper's name was even bandied about—but almost no one *really* cared. For most, it was just a freak show, a vivid explosion of excitement to an otherwise drab existence.

And while no one at the office came close to matching Charlie McGinty's belligerent callousness—there was no talk of this third victim constituting a hat trick—Nora still had to struggle through the day, thinking of Shannon all the while, barely holding her tongue at the most ignorant comments.

"It's awful," Nora said at dinner that night with Josh, the two sitting on opposite sides of the square, wooden dining room table, a white tablecloth covering the scratches below. "Three of them."

The other night's strong words were forgotten with the

sole exception of Nora knowing that she could never again compare Josh to his sister. He had even proven the unfairness of the comparison by cooking homemade lasagna with a tossed salad on the side because he'd seen her recent fatigue. It was a gesture Shannon had never made, had probably never even considered, and this was far from Josh's first time.

But it was impossible to stay away from the topic of the murders.

"I'm sorry, but those women disgust me," Josh said,

"What about the men?" Nora asked, then slid another morsel of the lasagna into her mouth, the tomato and cheese so delicious she knew she'd have to be careful or she'd devour it all night.

Josh raised an eyebrow. "The killers? Or killer?"

"No, not them. Well, of course, them. Or him. Of course, him, but I was talking about the customers. It takes two to tango. It's always the streetwalker who gets arrested—"

"Like Shannon."

"—never the customers. What about them?"

A thoughtful look crossed Josh's face as he shoveled a mouthful of lasagna in and chewed. "They disgust me, too."

Nora nodded as though she'd made a point.

"But mostly the whores," Josh said.

"Don't use that word."

"That's what they are. They disgust me." He paused as if unsure to continue. "Shannon, too. *Especially* Shannon."

"It's complicated."

"No it isn't. It's as black and white as can be."

"It's a gray world."

"You think Shannon is just a *gray* person?"

"She's a very loving girl. She just has problems."

Josh snorted. "Loving!" He shook his head in disgust.

"Yes, in her own way, she's a very loving girl."

"After what she's done to you? After what she's done to all of us? Are you serious?" Josh stared in disbelief. "I hear about her from some guys. You should hear the things they say. And I have to listen to it. About my own sister! And until she got locked up, she stole *everything*."

Nora had no answer for that.

"Remember my coin collection?" Josh asked. "Remember my full set of baseball cards from when I was seven? There were some valuable rookie cards in that collection. A signed Dustin Pedroia rookie card! All gone. She took *everything*!"

Again, Nora had no answer. The girl had taken her toll on all of them. Hell, maybe even Mark might not have looked for the "love of his life" if Shannon hadn't been making life at home so miserable.

They ate in silence for what felt like a long time, long enough at least for Josh to wolf down three helpings and her to feel frustrated that she had to stop at two.

"I'm staying over Eric's house tomorrow night, okay?" Josh asked. Eric was his best friend, also a good student and with parents that seemed nice enough.

"Yeah, sure," Nora said on autopilot, her mind stuck on Shannon's past transgressions and Josh's sweetness. "Thanks for making dinner."

"If I had less homework, I'd do it more often," he said with a smile. "But I could tell you needed it."

"Thanks, I'll clean up." Nora stood and grabbed her plate.

"No, let me," Josh said, his hand out in a stopping gesture. "Just sit on the couch and watch TV. Take it easy. Give me a holler in an hour and I'll bring you a bowl of chocolate chip ice cream."

"Oh, I've eaten more than enough," Nora said, and patted her too-ample stomach.

"You sure?"

"Oh, you know me. I'll probably holler and in less than an hour."

Josh grinned, and scooped up the plates.

"Thanks for being such a great kid," Nora said.

Josh smiled broadly. "Thanks for being such a great mom."

And as they both expected, she did give a holler half an hour later for that scoop of chocolate chip ice cream, adding "make it double."

There weren't many days that ended better.

———

A FOURTH PROSTITUTE was strangled and dumped on the Common down near the bandstand, and then a few weeks later, a fifth, left at the other end of the Common. Then a sixth in yet another random downtown location. And then a seventh just outside of Lynn Woods near the baseball field.

By that time, Boston-based TV news had taken notice, sending their roving reporters for live, on-site reports, and some blogger had taken to calling the killer The City of Sin Strangler, further cementing the "Lynn, Lynn, City of Sin" rhyme as the city's unfortunate call to fame. Unless, of course, the strangler would himself someday usurp that honor.

Nora didn't feel the icy fingernail of horror trace down her back until the eighth victim, a young woman whose body had not yet been discovered, a *potential* victim who was possibly not yet a victim. Nora had been tossing and turning in fits of sleep, her flannel pajamas growing damp with sweat until they clung to her skin, the darkness broken only by the red block numbers that read *3:13* on the clock radio on the nightstand.

Suddenly, Nora's eyes shot open with the dawning realization. Her mouth opened wide and a silent scream of agony erupted from deep within. Her mind, usually foggy when first coming out of sleep, instead showed her everything in pristine clarity.

It couldn't be. It just was not possible. She refused to believe it.

It was just a coincidence, one she hadn't noticed until now because...well, who would have even considered it, much less believed it? Certainly not her.

This *was* Josh, after all, the best kid a mother could ever hope for. It was insanity—a sort of parental blasphemy—to even consider the possibility.

But somewhere in the deepest, darkest recesses of her mind the tumblers had all fallen into place, and once fallen, they remained there.

The nights before all the most recent killings—God help her for even considering the possibility—were nights Josh had stayed over at Eric's house. Somehow, while she was sleeping, her nocturnal mind had done the computations, computations her daytime mind, the rational one, would not allow. She couldn't remember sleepover nights dating all the way back to the first killings months ago, but the most recent three she was certain of and she was pretty sure of the fourth. There'd been a pattern to his sleeping over— she allowed it on school nights because he was so conscientious—and that same pattern had followed the murders.

And Josh was sleeping over at Eric's house tonight.

Feeling cold sweat trickle down her back, Nora stared at the digital clock radio.

3:17

Well, if this insane hypothesis was really true—and surely, if there was a God in Heaven, it wasn't—but if it was, the poor girl, girl number eight, was most certainly already dead. The previous estimated times of death, at least those that had been announced, had always been within an hour or at most two of midnight. So for this victim, if this preposterous notion actually had any basis in reality—which was impossible—there was nothing Nora could do to help her, to reverse an abomination already performed.

Which, of course, didn't matter because it wasn't true. It couldn't be.

But if it was...what was she supposed to do?

There was no crime to stop. It was too late for that. She'd have to wait and see if an eighth body was discovered later this morning. And if it was, she'd have to confront Josh. Ask him to somehow explain this hellish coincidence. Tell him she didn't believe it, not one last bit of it, she would never, *ever* stop believing in his innocence. He was, after all, the greatest kid ever.

But if he could just provide a sliver of proof...

Of course, if all this nonsense was really true—and certainly it wasn't, it couldn't be, but if it was—and there was some chance that the girl was not yet dead but soon would be, didn't she have the obligation to contact the police so they could save the girl? Wasn't that her legal, moral, and ethical responsibility?

But the whole idea was *insane.* Her sweet son, the best kid *ever,* couldn't have done this. She couldn't contact the police with this absurd—hideous! indefensible!—idea, then if it was proven wrong—which it most certainly *had* to be!— just say oops, my mistake, with his impeccable reputation not just tarnished but *destroyed.*

He'd be humiliated, not just by the accusation that he was a serial killer, but what would be worse, infinitely worse, was that this untrue accusation *came from his own mother!*

Trembling, Nora sat back down on the bed. She stared at the bloodred numbers on the digital clock radio.

3:24

3:25

3:26

It was the longest night of her life.

———

THE LONGEST NIGHT became the longest day. All the local six a.m. newscasts opened with news—live from Lynn!—of an eighth prostitute, strangled and dumped downtown, this one outside a popular pizza parlor.

Nora stared at the TV screen in disbelief. Eight dead young women.

Eight. Dead. Josh.

Those three words did not belong together. The concept shouldn't compute. Couldn't compute.

But it did.

In a daze, Nora hurriedly dressed, not caring one whit if anything matched or the buttons lined up or anything— who gave a rat's ass!—and with her whole body shaking— breaking!—grabbed her keys and drove toward Eric's house, a mile and a half away but it felt like a hundred. She parked against the curb at the entrance to the dead-end street, gripping the steering wheel so hard her knuckles had turned white. The blue, split-level house with a garage and new, tan-colored shingles was a hundred yards away, the last house on the street butting up against a patch of oak trees, a rarity in this city. Nora sat wide-eyed, and waited.

When the boys finally emerged, she resisted the urge to shoot the Hyundai forward and instead approached slowly, as if *nothing* at all was wrong—nothing!—and her whole world didn't rely on what happened the next few seconds.

"Hey Josh, can you get in?" she said as soon as she pulled up alongside them, using as even a tone as she could manage. "Eric, I'll take him to school. I'd give you a lift, too, but we have a couple family things we have to discuss. Okay?"

Eric, all red hair and freckles, had looked like he was about to bolt, but Josh touched his arm, squeezed it, then calmly slid into the front seat beside her, closed the door, and said, "Sure, Mom, what's up?"

Cool as cucumber. Not a thing wrong.

Because of course, nothing *was* wrong. Jupiter had just aligned with Mars, or something like that, and there was a perfectly fine explanation for this...this most impossible of coincidences.

There had to be.

She made a U-turn, needing to get away from Eric and this house and anyone who could possibly be watching. She pulled out of the dead-end, turned right, then back into the next dead-end she could find, and up against the curb, all the while desperately trying to keep a lid on her boiling-out-of-control emotions.

"Josh," she said in a pleading tone she couldn't prevent, "could you please tell me, please just—"

She couldn't finish. The boiling-over emotions exploded, blasting the cover off, and she burst into tears, followed by spasms of wracking sobs. Sobs that shot stabbing pains into her side and chest. Wracking sobs of the darkest sorrow, unfathomably deep in its blackness.

She tried to choke back the sobs. Tried to speak. Tried to say the words she couldn't bring herself to utter.

Josh put a comforting hand on her shoulder, and for a brief moment Nora was sure there was a logical explanation. Knew there was one, and was ashamed she'd ever doubted the best kid *ever*. How could she have ever thought such a despicable thing about him?

And when the choking sobs and salty tears finally subsided, Nora dried her tears, blew her nose with a clean, folded handkerchief Josh handed her, and looked at her wonderful son, her pride and joy, and laughed at her foolishness. She'd been so silly. She'd been such a fool to even *begin* to ask.

And the best kid ever said, "Don't worry. We won't get caught."

The bottom fell out of Nora's stomach. Her head spun. She felt as though she were about to faint.

"Pull yourself together," Josh said softly, with a maturity in his voice of a man twice his age, squeezing her shoulder in a gesture that at any other time would have offered reassurance that everything would turn out right.

Nora stared into her son's eyes. Eyes she'd always thought of as soft brown. There was nothing soft about them now.

"Are you all right?" Josh asked gently, soothingly.

She nodded yes, but no, she was most definitely not all right. Had he really admitted that...no, he had to have meant something else. Admitted to playing hooky or...or getting drunk or...or something.

Even smoking pot. Or snorting cocaine. Even shooting heroin. *Anything!*

There was some explanation for this. There had to be. And afterward, Josh would say, incredulous, "You thought I meant *that*?" Because it was, of course, impossible. He'd be incredulous and then angry that she'd thought he meant *that*.

Angry and hurt and humiliated that his own mother —*she!*—had thought that he was...

He was...

Could she even say the words? Think the words?

A serial killer?

No, no, no. Josh, her sweet, loveable, considerate Josh, who made his bed and cleaned his room and cooked her lasagna and brought her a double scoop of chocolate chip ice cream on a night when she was just so damned tired she couldn't even move. He was *not* a serial killer.

"Mom," Josh said, and tilted her head so she had to look at him through her tear-filled, blurry eyes. "I'm all you've got."

Nora felt her heart spasm, as if a powerful fist had grasped hold of it and was squeezing. Squeezing the life out of her.

She couldn't breathe. Again, her head spun. She could hardly hold it up.

"Mom," Josh said as if from a great distance. "Pull yourself together. You don't want to attract attention."

Nora blinked. She jerked her head upright. Blinked some more. Rapidly, as if doing so could change the sight before her.

"I saw on the news," she said, and though it broke her heart to even say it, she still managed the one word in a disbelieving, croaking sob. "*You?*"

Josh nodded. Coolly, dispassionately. As if affirming that

he'd gotten his homework done that night. Or done the dishes. Or made his bed.

"But...*why?*"

"It's a cesspool out there. Somebody has to clean it up."

"But—"

"They're like a disease."

"But for some mother, those girls are their—"

"Yeah, their Shannon."

Once again, Nora felt her head swim. She couldn't swallow. Couldn't breathe.

When she could finally speak again, Nora said, "But she's your sister."

"*Exactly!*" Josh said, his voice cold and hard as steel on a winter day. "No more Shannons."

"I'll get you counseling," Nora offered, feeling like a drowning woman grasping at anything to stay afloat. "This isn't you. I won't say a thing as long as you change. Just talk to—"

"I don't need counseling. I know what I'm doing."

"But you have such a bright future. You can be anything you want."

"*This* is what I want."

"You can't mean that."

"I do. This is my life's work."

Nora shook her head. "No, no, no."

"If I became a doctor, would you be proud of me?"

Nora shook her head in confusion at the change of topics. "Of...of course."

"Then think of me as a doctor, specializing in cancer removal."

"This can't go on."

"It *must.*"

Nora couldn't think of anything to say. Couldn't think of anything to do.

"If you even think about doing something foolish, like telling *anyone*, even Dad, about this," Josh said, "just remember, I'm all you've got."

Nora nodded dumbly.

"You understand?" Josh asked.

She kept nodding.

And not knowing what else to do, she drove him to school.

———

NORA GOT through the next few days, robotically taking blood pressures and temperatures, entering the numbers on her tablet, verifying medical histories, and saying all the right things.

"Are you okay?" people would ask, and she'd say yes, she was fine, just a little tired, not sleeping well. And that much was true. She wasn't sleeping well. She was hardly sleeping at all, drifting off only to awake with a start, drenched in sweat, the nightmare still fresh and hideously vivid in her mind.

A nightmare in which Josh was strangling some poor girl, a young woman who had once been some mother's little baby, cradling her in her arms. Her pride and joy.

But Josh had wrapped that piece of rope around her throat and was pulling it tight as that poor girl's eyes bugged out.

While she, Nora, stood next to the girl.

Watching.

Doing nothing.

The only time the nightmare varied were the times the girl was Shannon.

———

THEY ATE dinner the next Tuesday night, a nice chicken stir-fry that Josh made for them, set out on a new checkered tablecloth he'd bought over the weekend. Only the clinking of the silverware on plates broke the silence between them.

"I'm going over to Eric's," Josh announced calmly as he stood to clear the table.

Nora couldn't breathe. She looked up at her son towering over her, his face impassive.

"No," she said, the only word she could manage.

"Yes," Josh said. "I'm not asking you. I'm telling you."

Nora tried to calm the hammering inside her chest. "But why?"

"It's easier over there."

In her mind's eye, she saw the single-family split-level at the end of a dead-end street butting up against a patch of trees. She understood that part.

"But why?" she repeated, the words the same but the question different.

"Because I have to."

"You can't keep doing this."

"We've discussed this before."

"You'll get caught. You'll spend the rest of your life in jail."

"No, we won't. We're smarter than the cops." Josh looked at her for long seconds. "The only thing that could stop us is..." He shrugged. "...you. Eric wanted to kill you as soon as you found out, but I wouldn't let him." Nora swallowed hard. Josh smiled. "I told him you'd never betray me. You can't. I'm all you've got."

Nora nodded dumbly.

"But just in case," he said, "give me your cell phone."

"Why?"

"Because we have no land line, and the cell is the one thing that could get you in trouble. In some spasm of guilt, thinking you could save some poor whore before we get to her, you might call the cops, call that anonymous number they've set up just to catch the City of Sin Strangler." He laughed at the media's nickname. "You might not be able to bear the thought of letting another whore like Shannon die. Any more than you can't bear the thought of turning me in after the deed is done. So give me your cell."

Robotically, as she'd performed so many actions in the past weeks, Nora went to the bedroom, fetched her cell where it was already charging on the nightstand, and handed it over to her son.

"Don't leave this house," Josh warned. "Don't step outside this apartment's front door. Eric's worried about you. He doesn't know just how much you love me." Josh smiled with an apparent warmth that would have filled Nora's heart with happiness back before everything changed. "He might leave me on my own tonight, come back here and make sure you don't leave this place. He says he'll have to kill you if you do.

"I'd hate to see that happen," Josh continued, "most of all because I love you." Again, he smiled. "But also because it would focus attention on me, and that would be very, very bad. It would point the cops right in my direction. And from me to Eric. It's really all that has stopped him. But if you step outside, he'll have no choice."

Josh waited for a reaction and when he got none, other

than what Nora supposed was her crazed, wild-eyed stare, he added, "Besides, by now, you're an accomplice. You've known and said nothing. You'd be turning yourself in along with Eric and me. Like it or not, you're part of the team."

He smiled, then headed into the kitchen and did the dishes, humming some unidentifiable tune as he worked. Washed the dishes, dried them, and put them back in the cabinets.

A good boy.

Nora remained seated at the table, frozen, staring at the checked tablecloth.

Josh came back into the room. "Gotta go, Mom. Love you."

He bent down and kissed her on the head.

"Don't go."

"Got to."

"You're all I've got."

"Then be proud. I'm cleaning the cesspool."

———

Nora kept staring at the checkerboard tablecloth long after he left, wishing it could somehow hypnotize her into a trance she never awoke from. Josh knew her all too well. Once a poor young woman was dead and nothing could bring her back to life, Nora couldn't bear to end her own son's life, too. What was to be gained by that?

He was right. He was all she had left. And nothing would bring those dead girls back.

Eight of them!

But he was also right that she couldn't bear to allow that number to grow to nine. Somewhere, that poor girl had a mother, just like Shannon had her, and Nora could not allow another one to die. No matter what it cost.

Feeling the weight of the world upon her shoulders, Nora stumbled into her bedroom and fished out an old shoe from the back of the closet. She tilted it, and out slid a black device she had hoped never to use.

Nora stared at the disposable cell phone she'd bought several days ago. Untraceable. The tool of drug dealers and crooks everywhere.

And now, a broken-hearted mother. Who would, by its use, lose the last good thing left in her life.

She'd memorized the toll-free number. Had told herself she'd never have to use it. Josh would stop. He'd listen to her. He'd always been such a good, good boy.

But no.

And so, this was it.

With hands shaking so uncontrollably she had to reenter three of the digits, Nora keyed in the numbers for the worst phone call in her life.

IN ANOTHER LIFE

INTRODUCTION TO "IN ANOTHER LIFE"

I'll admit it, I'm cheating here. This last piece of flash fiction doesn't perfectly fit any of the mystery, suspense, crime, or thriller categories. It's here mostly because I want it to be here, and I want you to read it.

I had a carefully thought-out, highly political rationalization for its inclusion, but I'm just going to let the story speak for itself.

"In Another Life" first appeared in *Flash Me Magazine*, and finished in second place in its Readers Choice Award.

IN ANOTHER LIFE

We sit, holding hands in the setting light, and watch the ducks glide peacefully through the air, squawking with airborne joy until they splash down to feast on breadcrumbs thrown by strangers. Beside us, squirrels run up the trees, circling them like the red stripe of a barber's pole, and then race back down.

In another life, we speak of our son's marriage and—using both words and our private language of shared thoughts, sideways glances, and gestures—observe that she isn't quite good enough for him. But who is? Who could be? We speak of our grandchildren and soccer games and honor rolls and science fairs. Of Little League, and birthday parties, and my, how they've grown.

In another life, we are babysitting those grandchildren so our son—such a loving boy, such a fine young man—can go out for the evening with his wife. We coax the little ones into throwing breadcrumbs in the water. When the ducks splash down and plunge their necks into the water, greedily gobbling up the crumbs and squawking for more, those innocent faces look up at us with carefree joy and laugh and laugh.

In another life, our son has returned to us, his chest thrust out proudly and festooned with medals, his shoulders straight, his sense of duty fulfilled. And even if he never fathers us grandchildren, we rejoice in his accomplishments, his joys, and his dreams still alive and vibrant.

Off to our right, a squirrel feverishly chases after another, up and down one tree and then another. Are they playing? Or is the one chasing the other, for some offense small or large, until it can catch it and kill it? In another life, we would believe they are playing.

One of us rests a head on the other's shoulder. One of us feels the other tremble, hears the muffled, choked sobs. And then we share that too.

THE INTERVIEW

INTRODUCTION TO "THE INTERVIEW"

With this story, we return to the T, Boston's subway system. Like the smell?

I might argue, however, that much of the story's heart is in Boston's financial district, and the story's soul lies in the divide between those who ply their trade there and punks like the one in the torn denim jacket you're about to meet.

Be forewarned that this story predates the advent of Uber, Lyft, and other such services. Please forgive that anachronism.

THE INTERVIEW

The punk in the torn denim jacket eyed Richmond Franklin up and down, then grinned. Richmond felt a spasm of icy fear slice through his belly even though at 6-2, 210 pounds, he had a good six inches and fifty pounds on the kid. Reflexively, Richmond tightened his grip on the handle to his Brunello Cucinelli leather briefcase, then touched the matching wallet he'd moved to his suit's breast pocket. Not much cash in it, barely two hundred. But there was his license and all the plastic with the five-figure credit lines.

He didn't belong here, standing in this filthy subway car that reeked of sweat and cheap perfume, packed so full of society's dregs he couldn't help brush against one of them for an appalling moment that made his flesh crawl. He'd pull away each time, of course, grimacing, wanting to brush away whatever traces they might have left on his Valentino tailored suit, Stefano Ricci striped shirt, or Salvatore Ferragamo tie. But one of them would bump into him again, repeating the episode every time the squealing car took a corner, rocking back and forth. Sometimes the lights would flicker out and he'd catch his breath, unable to exhale until they came back on.

These were not his smells, his sounds, his people. He belonged in a limo, one whose chauffeur provided each morning a steaming hot coffee (black, unflavored), a croissant (warm, with a thin layer of butter spread on top), and a *Wall Street Journal* (folded just once, with the headline facing up).

That was what Richmond Franklin—*Richmond*, not Rich, Dick, Richie, Rick, or Rickie, only *Richmond*—had always gotten. Had expected. Had deserved.

Until that bitch Carmela Santucci cut the legs out from under him that one Thursday afternoon in the board room, blindsiding him in front of not only Old Man Colson but the other eight vice presidents gathered about the polished walnut table, in theory Richmond's peers, but in practice no match for his intelligence, wit, deportment, and looks. He'd seen the rabid, breathless hunger in their eyes when Carmela Santucci took him down. It was the same eager look of expectancy that came across faces in crowds watching a potential suicide atop a high building, faces flushed in anticipation, hoping he'd jump.

Richmond Franklin had jumped and now...now, thanks to the cab driver strike, he was reduced to riding the subway with the vermin. Not for long, though. Today, he had hit a home run during the interview at Streeter, Charles, Stuart, and Smith. Knocked it out of the ballpark. Tomorrow they'd call him for a second interview that would be a mere formality, then make him an offer that topped his old compensation package and he'd be back riding limos and reading the *Wall Street Journal* instead of wading in this cesspool.

The punk grinned again. He was eighteen, twenty tops. Acne-scarred. Unruly dark, shoulder-length hair.

Richmond looked away. He counted to ten, watching the punk out of the corner of his eye while hoping it wasn't obvious. The punk didn't move. He just stood there, holding on to the floor-to-ceiling post with one hand, his other shoved into jeans as torn as his jacket, grinning beneath the advertisement for Booker, Ward, and Trust, Richmond's old investment firm. The stupid advertisement. Green dollar signs superimposed on a white background with George Washington, front and center, winking.

Carmela Santucci liked the dumb ad, dumb because it featured George Washington, the president on the *one-dollar* bill. In the old days, Richmond could have used a one-dollar bill for a napkin. For toilet paper, for crying out loud. And the firm was trying to sell its image based on that? They should have at least used Benjamin Franklin. Not a president, but on the one-hundred-dollar bill.

It was all about the Benjamins, not all about the Georges. But neither Carmela Santucci nor the other eight vice presidents would have understood that. Richmond thought, not for the first time, that it had been a stroke of luck that he'd been severed from all those unimaginative dolts, the whole lot just a bunch of sheep following Old Man Colson. Good riddance to the whole lot of them.

Richmond eyed the grinning punk, saw with relief that he hadn't moved, and when the screeching subway car stopped at Government Center, Richmond stepped down onto the dirty platform, sidestepping an empty Doritos bag and a pink, half-squished wad of bubblegum.

Richmond glanced over his shoulder and watched the punk join the rest of the crowd getting off the car, too. Icy tendrils crawled over Richmond's skin. The hair rose on the back of his neck as he gripped his Brunello Cucinelli brief-case tightly enough to turn his knuckles white. He hoped he didn't have to use it to defend himself. It would cost three grand to replace.

Deciding he'd make his stand here, in front of all these witnesses—the legend of Kitty Genovese be damned—he got to the Dunkin' Donuts kiosk with its line of only three people and whirled on the punk.

"What do you want?" Richmond said, trying for the toughest badass voice he could muster, the tone he'd used to emasculate rival after rival at Booker, Ward, and Trust. Back in the day.

The punk, who'd been trailing him, doing the pimp roll even though he was white, looked surprised but unruffled. Expensive new sneakers, Nikes. Brown eyes that seemed to be laughing at some joke that only he knew.

"I'd like to talk to you," the punk said.

People jostled about them, glancing at them in annoy-ance before seeing their faces and looking quickly away.

"About what?" Richmond asked, cool and disinterested.

"A private matter."

Richmond wished he wasn't carrying the briefcase. It kept him from crossing his arms and getting the body language advantage on the little snot. "I'm not going anywhere."

The punk spread his arms. "You don't gotta be afraid of me."

Richmond waited.

It would be a long wait. He'd long since learned the intimidation factor that silence provided. When he'd bought his Lexus, he'd just sat before the salesman and as soon as the negotiations started, had refused to speak.

"I got a business proposition," the punk finally said.

Richmond snickered. "*You* have a business proposition for *me*?"

"Yeah," the punk said, not backing off an inch. "Looks to me like you got axed a while back, am I right?"

That stopped Richmond.

"And you're still looking for a job, am I right?"

A single cold bead of sweat trickled down the side of Richmond's forehead. He wiped it away. "How do you know that?"

"You got the look." It wasn't a grin the punk flashed this time; it was a smirk. As more people brushed against the two of them, he nodded to the area behind the Dunkin' Donuts kiosk. "Now could we step over there and get some privacy?"

Richmond didn't accept terms like that. He *set* the terms; he didn't *accept* them. So he said, "No," and pointed to an equally private area past the escalator/stairs. No different really. Except that he held the upper hand now.

The punk grinned broadly. "Man, was I right or was I right?"

Richmond didn't like turning his back on the punk, but wasn't about to show even a hint of fear so he strode briskly to the first green and white column past the stairs, listening for any sudden movement behind him, ready to whirl and wield his Brunello Cucinelli as a shield while delivering a knee to the groin. But he heard only the screech of a subway car, felt only the moistening of his palms.

"I need a guy like you in my crew," the punk said, standing a good two strides away, making no effort to invade Richmond's personal space. "A guy who'll fit in with the Beacon Hill crowd, the upper crust, you know what I mean? Look good in a monkey suit like the one you got on."

Richmond fingered the lapels of his gray suit. "A monkey

suit? This is a Valentino. Custom tailored. It costs—" He stopped himself. It wouldn't pay to tell him how much a suit like this cost. It might encourage the punk to steal it, tear the clothes right off him. "It's the best suit you can buy."

"Yeah, a monkey suit," the punk said. "I need a guy just like you."

Richmond had to laugh. The punk was trying to hire *him*. "Take a hike."

———

STREETER, Charles, Stuart, and Smith made him an offer but it was a joke of an offer. Almost an insult. Richmond Franklin could no more accept it than he could entertain a client at McDonald's.

He'd thought it was an opening salvo in a negotiation. A lowball opening salvo, trying to sense weakness that wasn't there. Richmond Franklin hadn't gotten where he was by *ever* being weak.

So he called their bluff, showing them who really had the biggest stones, only it turned out it wasn't a bluff.

He'd waited a week for them to get back to him in response to his counteroffer and when the phone hadn't rung, Richmond had backed down and called them back, ready to say that his counteroffer was open to negotiation.

"I'm sorry, but after you rejected our offer we moved on," the female voice on the end of the line said. Amanda Something-or-Other. A sweet-sounding voice on the surface but with an undercurrent of the bloodthirsty victor. "The position is no longer available."

"But I thought—"

"Mr. Franklin, if I may be frank with you, there is a multitude of candidates out there. If you will allow me the metaphor, you're a dime a dozen. There are thousands of you out there now. This isn't like the old days."

"That was an idiom," Richmond said with a sneer.

"Excuse me?"

"That wasn't a metaphor. It was an idiom." And then Richmond added a few descriptive personal phrases about Amanda What's-Her-Name, phrases available to HBO but not the networks, and kept going even after the nastiest of them resulted in a dead phone line.

The weeks went by, and then the months.

Nibbles but no bites.

He plowed though his severance package and cash reserves almost overnight. Richmond began to notice costs he'd never noticed before. The two-hundred-dollar haircuts by Armando. He was the best, worth every penny, an invest-ment in Richmond's career when you thought about it. What else could he do, go to Supercuts?

There were the six-dollar hazelnut macchiatos every morning. The dinners at L'Espalier, Bistro du Midi, Clio, Deuxave, and La Morra. The pick-me-up trip to Vegas that he'd really needed to fortify his mental well-being. The list went on and on.

When the last of the cash reserves was gone, Richmond drew on his lines of credit, which lasted until the credit bureaus noticed the activity and before he knew what had happened, the bloodthirsty bastards had cut off all his remaining credit.

"I'm sorry," the secondary MasterCard account represen-tative said, his voice gravelly and deep, "but you've added an astonishing amount of debt in recent months—"

"I know how much debt I've added," Richmond snapped, wondering if the vermin on the other end of the line was really allowed to editorialize like that. An *aston-*

ishing amount of debt. That from a guy who'd never owned a Rolex, never driven a Mercedes, never lived on Beacon Hill. Richmond put the sharpest of steel in his voice. "If you give me a specified credit limit, then you should *honor* that credit limit. What's the point to a credit limit that's only available until I need to use it?"

Richmond winced. *Need.* That had been a slip.

"Sir, when we see a rapid escalation of debt, we must review the situation. Perhaps it would help if you could provide verification of your current employment."

"*What?*"

"Sir, when we first tried to contact you about our concerns, we called your office number at Booker, Ward, and Trust and were told that you no longer work there."

Silence.

This time the silence hung over Richmond, not the other way around. His hands began to tremble ever so slightly.

He closed his eyes.

"Mr. Franklin?" the voice on the other end of the line finally said.

Richmond Franklin softly hung up the phone.

———

DAY AFTER DAY, he headed for the subway, looking for the punk in the torn denim jacket with increasingly frantic desperation. It took almost two weeks.

"Hey, I was hoping to see you," Richmond said, flashing his most winsome smile, his deal-closing smile, when he finally spotted the punk.

He was wearing the same torn denim jacket, though it

was a good deal more worse for the wear than the last time. Same acne scars and shoulder-length dark hair.

The punk eyed him coldly. "Yeah."

"That business opportunity you mentioned to me a few months ago..."

"Yeah?"

Richmond shrugged, trying hard to appear nonchalant. "I might be interested after all."

The punk nodded. "What changed your mind?"

Richmond licked his lips. His mouth felt dry, his chest tight. "Some other...opportunities...haven't worked out for me."

The punk grinned. That warmed Richmond's heart. Now to close the deal.

"So if you just give me an idea of the parameters," Richmond said.

"Parameters?"

"Yes," Richmond said. "The details."

"You could find yourself on the wrong side of the law," the punk said.

Richmond nodded, a little too eagerly at first. "From white collar crime to blue collar." He laughed nervously, then felt silent as soon as he heard its false tone.

"What if you had to, like, sell some X to some high school kids? Could you do that?"

Richmond's heart sank. He'd been afraid of this. He hated to stoop this low, but what else could he do? The last of the credit card companies had cut him off. Maybe one quick strike and he'd get out. One or two. Just to keep himself solvent until he lined up something else. Something else was bound to turn up soon. He licked his lips and drew in a deep gulp of air.

"I...I suppose I could. I thought you wanted me for

something more attuned to my skills, but if that's what it takes..." After all, the punk wasn't asking him to murder anyone. If some dope in high school wanted a thrill, who was he to stop him? Richmond found himself nodding so eagerly he'd almost turned himself into a bobble-head doll. He stopped himself. "I guess I could do that."

"You guess?"

"I can do it," Richmond said, hating the panic in his voice but unable to stop it. "I know I can do it. Give me a shot. Let me prove myself. You won't regret it."

It was just the way Richmond remembered it. The stench of terrible need, given away by the catch in the throat, the dry mouth, the nervously shifting eyes. Just like the old days. Only this time he was on the other side, no longer watching with distaste while the subject squirmed. Now he *was* the subject and he hated it.

The punk's eyes narrowed. "You'd do that? Sell to kids?" His voice was hard and cold.

Richmond blinked. "What? I thought—"

"That was a test."

"A test?"

"You failed."

"But I was just trying—"

"You think I need a guy like you to sell X? I thought you was smart. Confident. A tough guy in a monkey suit. I thought you had balls. But you ain't smart. You ain't none of that. You know what you are?"

Richmond cringed, sure that he didn't want to hear the answer.

"You're just like a crack whore."

"I don't do—"

"Just as desperate. I don't need desperate. I need cool.

Aloof. I need someone who'll make the business come to him...someone who can drive a hard bargain."

"That's me," Richmond said, his heart hammering. "I've done that for years. I get a guy's balls in my hands and squeeze." Richmond smiled as he thought back to those good old days. "That's me. I'm the guy you need."

The punk shook his head. "Nah. That *was* you. That guy I'd hire. But you? You're useless to me. You're just another crack whore. Without the crack."

Richmond started to ask what that meant, but stopped. His broad shoulders inside his finely tailored Valentino suit slumped, and his heart sank. He could do the math.

DEATH IN THE SERENGETI

INTRODUCTION TO "DEATH IN THE SERENGETI"

Like so many other stories in this collection, "Death in the Serengeti" came from the opportunity to write for a themed anthology. In this case, *New York Times* bestseller Kevin J. Anderson was looking for thriller short stories. Thrillers, by their very nature, tend to demand a lot more words than the 6,000 he allotted, but that was the challenge. And a formidable one it was.

I finished my first attempt a day before the deadline, and showed it to my wife, Brenda. I am the luckiest guy in the world to share my life with her, but she is not what one would call a critical reader. Her reactions are almost always positive.

(Although there was that one time when she told me she kept getting into the story and then I would veer off unpredictably into another direction, after which she'd be getting into the story again only to have me veer off in that same totally confusing fashion. "I don't understand what you're doing," she confessed. We finally realized that for the first time, I had printed the story double-sided, and she'd been reading only the odd-numbered pages.)

Brenda's reaction to my thriller short story, an intensely personal one, was surprisingly negative. Especially for her.

"I think this is a thriller for you," she said cautiously, "but I don't think it's a thriller for anyone else."

She was, of course, spot on. Hit the bull's-eye. I was so close to the story, and it was so personally traumatic, I couldn't see that it wasn't a thriller at all.

What could I do? It was early Saturday evening and the hard deadline was Sunday midnight, Pacific Time, so three a.m. for me on the East Coast.

I got to thinking and soon had one of those slap-your-head moments. A year earlier, we had gone on the trip of a lifetime to Africa. Why wasn't I putting my thriller short story in that exotic setting instead of drab old Boston? Weren't there an abundance of thriller ideas in Africa? For an allegedly smart guy, I'm often really, really dumb.

I got pounding the keys that Saturday night, slept, then resumed early Sunday morning. I wrote like a madman, taking only bathroom breaks, eating at my desk. I loved the story I was telling, but that three a.m. deadline loomed ominously.

I kept writing. The clock kept racing.

It looked like the clock would win.

I wrote the final scene all but holding my breath while my brain silently screamed, "Oh baby, oh baby, oh baby! *Hurry!*" I copied the file from my no-Internet writing computer to a flash drive, raced to my laptop, ran spell check, and pushed the send button on the email at 2:58 a.m.

If the story itself wasn't a thriller, the writing of it certainly was.

Kevin J. Anderson *loved* the story, but I almost broke out laughing when he commented that the final scene felt a little rushed. Rushed? He had no idea!

Kevin then made the extraordinary gesture of offering to sit down at lunch and brainstorm ideas of possible ways to make it even better. Amp up the tension even more. Over Thai food in Lincoln City, Oregon, he and I and another writer discussed my story and the other writer's story.

It was a terrific learning experience. A view into the mind of a bestselling writer.

We had to discard anything that added to word count because the anthology length was already running hot. So we couldn't consider actually showing what happened after the current ending or pursuing some interesting tangential explorations of character.

In the end, the word-count straitjacket forced me to tighten the writing in one scene before I could add extra words in another. And I needed those extra words to get the resonance of a back story between the two main characters. (I also had to tweak the "rushed" final scene.)

Perhaps that word-count straitjacket helped make the story as successful as it became. Perhaps it was a better story for the tightening, and I was fortunate I hadn't been granted an extra five hundred or a thousand words. Or perhaps the success was going to happen anyway. I don't know.

But what a great opportunity to witness a bestselling writer in action. I'm indebted to Kevin for his time and the learning experience. It amped up the story, and it amped up me.

"Death in the Serengeti" first appeared in *Fiction River: Pulse Pounders: Adrenaline*. To my astonishment and delirious delight, it was then reprinted in *Best American Mystery Stories, 2018*, edited by Louise Penny, series editor Otto Penzler. It also earned the 2018 Derringer Award for Best Long Story.

Getting one of my stories into a year's best anthology

had been a lifelong dream, and Penzler's had been my own personal favorite almost since its first appearance in 1997. Winning a best story award was another lifelong dream.

Two dreams come true with this one story.

I guess it's a good thing I pressed send on that email at 2:58 am instead of 3:01.

DEATH IN THE SERENGETI

THE SMELL OF newly rotting flesh hit Jakaya Makinda. He stopped his Land Rover, grabbed his binoculars off the seat beside him, and trained them in the direction of the odor's source.

Eighty meters away, mostly hidden by a rocky outcropping of man-sized boulders, lay the carcasses of a dozen or more slaughtered elephants.

Poachers.

Anger coursed through Makinda. He grabbed his Remington pump-action shotgun, and with his broad-brimmed hat shielding his eyes from the early morning sun, used the binoculars to scan the Serengeti's tall grass for predators. The poachers were long since gone, but he wasn't some damned fool white tourist, stepping out of the security of his vehicle, thinking how cute the animals were, all set to launch into "Hakuna Matata."

Out here, humans were food. Short and wiry, he'd be less of a meal than the overweight Americans whose entry fees paid his salary as Senior Park Ranger, but he had no interest in being any creature's gristly lunch.

He approached the rocky outcropping cautiously, binoculars dangling from his neck, his shotgun ready and his .38 holstered but loaded.

His stomach gave way when he stepped past the two largest boulders and saw the full extent of the carnage. Beside what had to be close to twenty dead elephants, their missing tusks sawn off at the roots, lay the carcasses of five hyenas, three jackals, and a couple dozen vultures.

The poachers, as they'd come to do, had poisoned the elephants with cyanide, killing them and everything that came to feast on their corpses, most importantly the vultures who wouldn't be left circling overhead for rangers such as himself to notice. The poison killed everything in its path, but made for an easier getaway.

Makinda gripped his shotgun tightly. He'd get these devils, these parasites who'd invaded even the Serengeti, Tanzania's greatest treasure. He'd get them if it was the last thing—

Behind him, his Land Rover exploded.

The force of the concussion knocked Makinda face-forward onto the ground. He tasted the tall grass in his mouth. Felt grains of the hard soil between his fingers. His ears rang.

He looked back over his shoulder and saw flames shooting up from the wrecked carcass of his vehicle. Makinda stared in disbelief and horror.

———

MAKINDA SHOT TO HIS FEET, grasping the shotgun, and ran toward the flaming wreckage of the Land Rover. He didn't know why. It was useless to him now. The two-way radio, referred to by safari companies as the "bush tele-graph," would be destroyed as was its backup.

He hadn't called in the slaughter because he knew the safari companies listened in on the rangers' frequency and would flock to this less-popular section of the park to gawk at the butchery. Makinda had wanted to report this in person back at HQ and shield tourists from the ugliness. Let them think Tanzania was perfect.

So now, he was stranded.

Alone.

And with no cell phone coverage in this sector of the Serengeti, there was now no way to reach the other rangers. No way to alert them that a group of poachers bold enough to blow up his vehicle weren't settling for elephant tusks. They'd be going for the staggering rewards of rhinoceros horns, which made those from elephant tusks pale by comparison.

Ever since that damned Vietnamese politician claimed rhino horn powder had cured his cancer, demand had shot through the roof faster than Makinda's head would have if he'd remained in the Land Rover. The street value now of an average-sized rhino horn was a quarter of a million dollars, and not surprisingly, rhino poaching deaths had skyrock-eted every bit as furiously, though mostly outside of the protected national parks. Even so, in this sector of the Serengeti, there were only seven rhinos left.

Makinda had always declined the thinly veiled bribe offers no matter how they escalated. He could be a wealthy man right now, retired in dirty luxury at the age of thirty-nine instead of struggling to care for both his own family of six and that of his late brother, Jephter, whose wife and seven children, Makinda had, of course, taken in.

The only time the temptation had come close to overwhelming him was when Jephter had lain dying of cancer in a Bunda clinic, and a poacher, a fat, white American with a Southern drawl named Luther Ricker, had whispered in his ear, "Save your brother. We'll give you enough of the rhino powder to make him well. You need not dirty your hands with our money, but save your brother."

Makinda knew the claims of the rhino powder's powers were nonsense; all the scientists here said it was so. But he had almost given in that one time.

And perhaps he should have, he sometimes thought. The experts weren't always right.

Makinda spat, trying to rid the bitter taste of that memory from his mouth. As the smell of burning metal and electronics filled the air, he struggled to gather his thoughts. His vehicle's explosion had only been the opening gambit. The rhinos would be next, if not his fellow rangers, and he couldn't just stand by and allow either group to be wiped out.

He had to move. Predators be damned, he had to get to some group that would help him contact his fellow rangers. He'd warn them and get them to the watering holes where the rhinos would be visiting, easy targets for the poachers if not protected.

Makinda had taken no more than five steps up the road when far to the north a soft explosion sounded. Distant and muted, little more than a "poof."

But unmistakable.

The hairs on the back of Makinda's neck stood up.

The north. Rashidi. That was where Makinda's top assistant was supposed to be this morning. Near the big hippo watering hole.

"No..." Makinda groaned.

But maybe, he thought, it hadn't really been an explosion. It had just been his overactive imagination, over-wrought at barely escaping his own death. It couldn't—

A second explosion echoed off to the west.

The West. Another soft "poof."

That would be Samson.

If Makinda was right, and in his suddenly nauseous gut he knew he was right, that left only Brayson, Salim, and Philipo. Brayson in the Northwest, Salim in the East, and Philipo in the South.

In rapid fire, soft explosions echoed off to the East and South.

Poof! Poof!

The taste of bile filled the back of Makinda's throat. Salim and Philipo. Makinda closed his eyes and waited for the fifth and final explosion.

Brayson's. The one that would complete the elimination of Makinda's entire staff. Wipe out their entire sector. Sure, there were many other rangers in the Serengeti, but that covered almost fifteen thousand square kilometers. Their sector was isolated.

They were on their own. Just him and Brayson.

Makinda waited, but the fifth explosion didn't sound. Had he missed it? If it had detonated simultaneously with his own, as had perhaps been the plan for them all, he'd have never heard it.

But Makinda's instincts told him otherwise. When the fifth explosion never sounded, he knew it had not come simultaneously with his own.

Brayson was a traitor.

———

HE HAD SOLD THEM OUT, the son of a bitch.

Makinda began to run down the road, shotgun slung over his shoulder and binoculars jangling about his neck. His boots clopped noisily, kicking up dirt in his wake. He didn't care if he had to run a hundred miles. When he got to Brayson, he'd throttle the traitor's sweaty, grime-covered throat and squeeze until Brayson's greedy eyes popped out.

If he was guilty.

One look, and Makinda would know for sure. But with a sinking, angry heart, he knew already. Brayson liked the night life too much. Handsome. Too handsome for his own good. A ladies' man. A gambler. A drinker and maybe more. Trekking off to Mwanza whenever he had two straight days off.

The appetites that gave birth to greed. And the murders of Rashidi, Samson, Salim, and Philipo.

And the attempt on Makinda himself that would have been successful if not for Makinda's lucky discovery of the butchered elephants, almost totally hidden from the road with the usually telltale circling vultures instead lying dead in the field.

A greed with no conscience.

In retrospect, it was obvious. Brayson had betrayed them all.

He'd betrayed himself.

Makinda picked up the pace, and in no time, his effort was rewarded.

A cloud of dust appeared on the horizon. Makinda stopped, and broke into a smile. A lucky break! Not a long shot, but still a much quicker arrival of a safari group than he could have expected.

He jumped up and down, ignored the jostling of the shotgun on his shoulder, and began to wave wildly with both hands. It wasn't exactly dignified behavior befitting a

Senior Park Ranger, but he didn't give a damn. He'd get them to stop even if he had to shoot out the tires, though that shouldn't be necessary. Any safari company's driver would know to stop for a clearly identified Park Ranger.

But when he peered through the binoculars, Makinda's smile faltered. His hands fell to his sides.

Something was wrong. He couldn't pinpoint exactly what from this distance, but something about the vehicle looked wrong.

Makinda dropped into a crouch and sprinted for the brush. He spotted a meter-high boulder, diagonally ahead to his right. He made a beeline for it, bent over double all the way, then continued away from the oncoming Land Rover and back to where the wreckage of his own vehicle still smoldered.

He dove behind another large boulder, tasted the tall grass once again and a bit of dry soil as well, and scrambled around to face the dirt road. His belly lay flat on the ground, the binoculars uncomfortably pinned against his lower ribcage. He readied the shotgun, touched his finger to the trigger, and tried to calm his hammering heart.

The Land Rover that approached looked different from those of all the safari companies he'd ever seen in the Serengeti. It still had the elevated roof that allowed tourists to stand on their seats, poke their heads out, and shoot photographs. Three African men stared out from just such a perch.

But they didn't hold cameras or binoculars. They held AK-47s.

The side windows were darkened. Makinda couldn't see if more compatriots of the men brandishing the AK-47s sat below or if the space was instead filled with cargo. Elephant tusks. Rhino horns.

A bitter taste again filled Makinda's mouth. He wanted to shoot now and ask questions later, but one pump-action shotgun against at least three AK-47s didn't sound like good odds to him, even if he got off the first two shots.

Makinda released the pressure of his finger on the trigger. Realized he was holding his breath. Exhaled slowly and as quietly as he could manage.

They stopped twenty meters short of what was left of his ruined vehicle: tortured, blackened steel with wisps of black smoke curling up from it.

Four men climbed out, three slender Africans, though none of them looked Tanzanian, and Luther Ricker, the fat American who'd tried to corrupt Makinda with the words, "Save your brother." All of them wore nondescript, long-sleeved khaki shirts and matching trousers and boots. One of the Africans wore a dark blue baseball cap. They all carried an AK-47 as they walked to the wreckage of Makinda's vehicle.

"Nice work," Ricker said in his Southern drawl, the "nice" long and drawn out. *Niiice.* It sent a chill up and down Makinda's spine. "You blew this one to kingdom come. He's having a little talk with Jesus right now. With Jesus and his brother." Ricker laughed, setting off waves of stomach fat rolling.

Makinda's finger tightened on the trigger.

"I don't see him," the African with the baseball cap said in Swahili.

"English!" Ricker yelled.

The man repeated what he'd said, this time in English.

"You vaporized the sucker!" Ricker said. "Blew him into *tiiiny* bits of dust. That's all that's left of him."

"No blood?" the African said.

"You think he survived this blast?" Ricker said in a tone

Makinda associated with talking to children and stupid people. "You want to look for his severed head, be my guest. But get your scrawny ass back here in three minutes. I ain't got no time for trophy hunting. We got some money to make."

Ricker lumbered back to their Land Rover and slid in the driver's seat, on the right, the near side facing Makinda. The three Africans looked at each other, gave slight shrugs, and loaded back into their vehicle.

"That better be all of them," Makinda whispered to himself long after they were gone. "If there's a separate group for each ranger they took out..."

He didn't want to think about that. Four against one was bad enough odds.

Although he knew it was worse than that. Much worse.

Four plus Brayson against him. Four AK-47s plus whatever Brayson was carrying now against one pump-action shotgun and a .38.

A Land Rover, actually two counting Brayson's, against a man walking on foot.

He didn't stand a chance.

Makinda started walking. After ten steps, he began to run.

———

AFTER THREE KILOMETERS, Makinda finally got lucky. Sweat ran in his eyes. His feet felt like he was walking on eggshells; his boots were not meant for running. His shirt was dripping wet.

But he'd only encountered a half dozen giraffe, a heard of about twenty elephants, and a hundred or so impalas of one variety or another. None of them had shown him any interest.

He'd pushed to get to a particular intersection of the dirt roads, knowing it was likely some safari group would pass it soon.

And he was right.

He was there at the crossing for less than two minutes when he spotted clouds of dust in the East billowing up from the road. Makinda considered wading into the tall grass far enough to hide himself until he was sure it was Nikons and Canons that were pointing out of the tops of the vehicles, and not AK-47s, but he figured he'd take his chances with the Land Rover over whatever hidden surprise waited for him in the tall grass.

As it turned out, it was an Ace African Safaris Land Rover, driven by Chibuzo Akunyili, a man Makinda had dealt with for years and called Chi. Makinda waved him down.

"What's up, Chief?" Chi said. "What are you doing out here all alone?"

"Hello, Chi. May I step inside? I've got a private message I need to give you."

Makinda liked Chi and thought he could trust him, but knew that what he was about to say would not be popular. He couldn't imagine any driver taking off and leaving him standing there – there'd be Hell to pay if anyone did – but the morning's events had shaken him. Makinda was taking no chances.

"Sure, hop in."

Makinda stepped aboard, and quickly introduced himself to the five tourists arrayed on three rows of blue seats, the first two rows consisting only of a single seat on each side, the last row the only one that stretched from side to side.

Sweat dripping off his face, he ducked down to speak to Chi, seated on the right side, the driver's side, of course. On the left was a large flyswatter to nail the occasional tsetse fly and a brown cardboard box filled with a dozen or so white boxed lunches.

"I've got a very dangerous situation here," Makinda whispered to Chi. "I need your complete discretion."

Chi's brow furrowed. "Of course." He was a broad-shouldered man of about fifty-five with short, gray hair. A white nameplate with black printing identified him at the front of the vehicle; a smaller one hung above the left pocket of his dark green shirt.

"You can't tell anyone about this," Makinda said. "My life depends on it. Possibly others." He pointed to the two-way radio and the square black microphone that hung from a chrome metal clip. "Nothing on the bush telegraph. It's going to be difficult, but I'm counting on you."

Chi nodded vigorously. "What's wrong?"

"I've got to commandeer this vehicle."

"Jakaya, these tourists paid top dollar! I can't—"

"Mine got blown up by poachers. I was supposed to be in it."

Chi fell silent.

"How many vehicles in this group you're hosting?" Makinda asked.

"Three. Four including this one."

"I need you to find them right away. We need to offload these people into those other three vehicles. Do you know where they are?"

"Sure. The other three are less than a kilometer away from here. They're viewing a pride of lions another group found. All of us heard on the bush telegraph and went rushing to join them. We were the farthest away. We're the last group getting there."

Makinda swore. He closed his eyes tightly. "Get going while I think."

The Land Rover lurched forward along the uneven dirt road.

"I can't have this going out over bush telegraph," Makinda said. "Not from you or any of the other drivers in your group. Or for that matter, any of the drivers in the other groups with other safari companies that will wonder why we're offloading people from this vehicle to the other three. Nothing can look unusual. Nothing can look suspicious."

"We can't offload people with lions out there," Chi said.

"I know. I know. How many other safari companies are already at the site?"

Chi got back on the two-way radio and asked.

"Close to a dozen," came the static-filled answer in Swahili.

Makinda shook his head. "We can't make the offload there. It's too dangerous. Besides, we can't let that many other drivers see us. The bush telegraph will talk about nothing else. The wrong ears will hear it." He squeezed Chi's shoulder tight. "Surprise is the only thing I have on my side."

Chi got Ace African Safari's other three drivers on the radio. "Problems with my vehicle. Bad differential. Rendezvous with me a half kilometer down the road, due East."

He hung up. "They're not happy. Two were in prime viewing position. They're going to get an earful over this for days. But they're coming. And they'll be quiet. I said the magic words."

"Bad differential?"

Chi nodded. "Bad differential is our code for silence."

Makinda nodded. "Thank you."

"After we ditch the cargo," Chi nodded toward the back, "do you need a driver?"

"I couldn't ask. This is too dangerous."

"Do you need a driver?"

"I believe these poachers killed four other rangers and would have killed me if I wasn't lucky. I probably won't get out of this alive. If you join me, you'll be every bit as much at risk."

"These poachers. They're going after the black rhinos?"

Makinda hated the name "black rhino." There was almost no color difference between the "white" and "black" variants, but the names had been given to the two species by the colonialists—based on the white version being more docile and the black more savage—and the racist titles had stuck. But now wasn't the time to quibble.

"I'd bet my life on it," Makinda said.

"Double that wager. Count me in."

———

THEY HEADED NORTHWEST, toward the last noted location of the nearest rhino. Makinda filled him in on all the details. If the man was going to die, he had a right to know. Chi drove with a sense of unspeakable fury over the pitted dirt roads, bouncing the two of them wildly in the air, straining at their seat belts every time he hit a pothole or partially submerged rock at top speed.

But they arrived too late for the first rhino.

Vultures circled overhead. Others filled a nearby tree. Flies swarmed through the air. The smell of blood and death was palpable.

The fallen rhino lay on its side, the armor of its lower torso blown apart by what must have been a shotgun blast at pointblank range, its horns hacked from its mighty head. Makinda stared at the magnificent creature. Almost four meters long and well over a thousand kilos.

Its only natural enemy: humans.

Humans and their greed and stupidity.

Makinda thought that if the Vietnamese politician were here right now—the one responsible for stoking the fires of this poaching greed—Makinda would shoot the man with no remorse at all.

———

THEY CAME UPON a second felled rhino, its midsection blown apart and its horns hacked off just like its brother.

And then a third.

Each time Makinda and Chi found the carcass further northwest than the one before. The guiding hand, of course, was Brayson's. No one else, not even the best of the safari tour guides, could have told the poachers where to find the rhinos so quickly.

Makinda spat on the ground, then they headed further northwest.

Soon, they saw vultures flying overhead and followed them to where fifteen more slaughtered elephants lay, huge holes ripped in their heads by shotgun blasts. Their tusks had, of course, been sawn off.

"I thought you said they used cyanide on the other elephants," Chi said. "Why shotguns now?"

"It's faster," Makinda said. "They think I'm dead along with all the other rangers, other than their buddy, Brayson, of course. There's no need to cover your tracks if there's no one left to catch you."

As if to underscore his point, a chorus of gunshots boomed in the distance. Makinda stared in that direction, then connected the dots of each slaughter in the map inside his mind.

Suddenly, Makinda knew the poachers' destination.

The tiny airstrip.

He hadn't expected that. He'd assumed that the poachers would exit the country using the same vehicle, taking no chances, sticking to back roads, staying as invisible as possible, and finding some unguarded path out of the country. Or use a standard exit point where there was a corrupt guard.

But via the airstrip? To get out of the country? The more he thought about it, the more sense it made, flying low beneath radar detection, especially if their destination was somewhere beyond one of the neighboring countries.

It was a tiny airstrip with a short, dirt runway suitable only for prop planes, so remote that it had once had a plane crash because a hippo had wandered onto the strip. It serviced only a handful of planes each day, if that.

"While they harvest those tusks," Makinda said, "we'll race to the airstrip. That's where they're going. I'm sure of it. If we're lucky, we'll get there first."

"Chief," Chi said hesitantly. "They've still got all the AK-47s. We've got one shotgun and a revolver."

Makinda explained his plan.

Chi stared at him. "Really?"

———

MAKINDA AND CHI WAITED, hiding in the thick trees that lined the short, six-hundred meter, dirt runway and its grass curtain. They crouched on one knee at the opposite end from where a small, nondescript, white bush plane rested beside the tiny white, wooden shack that serviced the airstrip. Other than the buzzing of insects and the chirping of birds in the trees around them, the place appeared lifeless. Not a soul was visible, although presumably someone was working in the shack, the same person whose battered old Jeep was parked outside, the lone vehicle visible in the open grassy area that passed for a parking lot.

Makinda and Chi had hidden their Land Rover a short distance past the airstrip, then raced back, crouching low and working around to their current position, not quite at the end of the strip on the opposite side from the Jeep and the shack, always staying under the cover of the trees.

In an ideal world, Makinda thought, he would arrest these men and bring them to justice along with Brayson. He would look directly into the eyes of Ricker, whose sadistic words, "Save your brother" haunted him still.

But a host of AK-47s against a single shotgun and a .38 didn't amount to an ideal world. He'd be lucky if he got any kind of justice at all.

Makinda was starting to wonder if he'd been wrong and the airstrip wasn't the poachers' destination after all when they drove up in their Land Rover and parked haphazardly next to the Jeep. The four men emerged, Ricker and the three Africans, AK-47s at their sides, shielded from view of the shack.

Makinda trained his binoculars on them as they walked single file into the shack. A solitary cry of outrage rang out briefly, then was silenced a split second later as the AK-47s roared to life.

Moments later, while Ricker strolled casually to the plane, unlocked it, and pulled down the stairs, the three Africans returned to the Land Rover. They unloaded stacks of curved, white elephant tusks, then carried them to the plane and stuffed them inside, angling the longer ones around the corner of the door. It took several trips for the three men until finally, the one in the blue baseball cap carried a green, blood-stained duffle into the plane and with the four poachers all aboard, closed the door.

"The duffle has the rhino horns," Makinda said. "I'm sure of it."

As the propeller blades whirled, he peered into the binoculars, needing to see inside the cabin, and muttered, "Good!" when he saw Ricker in the pilot's seat.

His assumption had been correct. There were no innocents aboard. Only the four poachers. It was time to make them pay for the deaths of the four rangers and whomever they'd just shot in the shack. For the butchered rhinos and the elephants. It was time to make sure they never returned to kill again.

"This revolver isn't going to do squat," Chi said.

"Aim for the propeller blades. Give it a chance."

The plane accelerated down the runway, at first moving at barely more than a standstill, then faster, speeding closer and closer to the two men waiting in ambush.

The plane roared, drowning out all sound, its propellers a blur.

Makinda tasted bile at the back of his throat. His heart hammered, but he felt strangely at peace.

"Come get it," he said, his voice steady.

The plane drew closer. Almost on top of them.

It began to take off, angling upward.

"Three... two... one," he said.

It lifted off the ground.

"Now!" Makinda yelled.

They burst out of their cover, firing. Makinda's shotgun boomed its deafening blast and the pilot-side window blew out. He pumped in another round, thinking he heard the ping of Chi's shot hit the thin metal of a propeller, then Makinda fired again, this time ripping a hole in the bush plane's white underbelly as it drew beside them.

Makinda pumped and fired, pumped and fired, aiming at the fuel tank as the plane shot past.

It wobbled at eye level, wings dipping wildly, groaned, then righted itself, inching higher off the ground.

He pumped and fired. Pumped and fired.

But the plane continued to climb.

Fifteen feet off the ground.

Twenty, then thirty.

And just when it appeared that they had failed, the plane fell silent. At first, Makinda, his ears ringing from the shotgun blasts, didn't realize it except on some subconscious level.

He pumped and fired, having long since lost count of the shots, but sure the Remington's external magazine was almost spent. He pumped and fired even as the plane stalled and then plummeted, nose down.

It crashed and just as Makinda and Chi both fired one last shot, the plane exploded violently, the concussion knocking the two men backward through the air.

A fiery ball shot high into the sky from the mangled wreckage of the plane. The smell of burning fuel and human flesh filled the air.

After a time, Makinda turned to Chi and hollered. "You up for a visit to Brayson's house?"

Chi nodded. "Wouldn't miss it for the world."

ALSO BY DAVID H. HENDRICKSON

Novels

Bubba Goes for Broke

Cracking the Ice

Offside

Offensive Foul

Collections

Shimmers and Laughs: Eight Wildly Hilarious Tales

Short Stories

Tiffany Gets her Boobs (FREE for a limited time)

Blue Note Heaven

All Over Again

Feline Masterpiece

Drawing Dead

My Dark Angel

Baby, One More Time

Beloved

Nonfiction

How to Get Your Book into Schools and Double Your Income with Volume Sales

Travis Roy: Quadriplegia and a Life of Purpose

Writing as D. H. Hendrickson

(Hockey Romance Novels)

Novels

Body Check

No Defense

Short Stories

Shooting for the Moon

ACKNOWLEDGMENTS

To Kris Rusch and Dean Wesley Smith for breathing life into my writing career.

To Kevin J. Anderson for the eye-opening brainstorming session over Thai food.

To Louise Penny and Otto Penzler for selecting "Death in the Serengeti" for *Best American Mystery Stories 2018*, fulfilling a lifelong dream.

To the Short Mystery Fiction Society for bestowing the Derringer Award for Best Long Story on "Death in the Serengeti," fulfilling yet another lifelong dream.

To my editor, Dayle Dermatis, whose expertise saves me from myself so many times.

To all my family and friends who have supported me.

And, of course, to The Kid, my amazing wife Brenda, who makes it all possible and worthwhile.

David H. Hendrickson's first novel, *Cracking the Ice*, was praised by *Booklist* as "a gripping account of a courageous young man rising above evil." He has since published five additional novels, including *Offside*, which has been adopted for high school student required reading. He expects to release the first book in a new mystery series in late 2019 or early 2020.

His short fiction has appeared in *Best American Mystery Stories 2018*, *Ellery Queen's Mystery Magazine*, *Heart's Kiss*, multiple issues of *Pulphouse*, and numerous anthologies, including over a half dozen issues of *Fiction River*. He is a multi-finalist for the Derringer Award, and his story "Death in the Serengeti" was honored with the 2018 Derringer Award for Best Long Story.

Pentucket Publishing released his first short story collection, *Shimmers and Laughs: Eight Wildly Hilarious Tales*, in 2018. This is his second short story collection.

Hendrickson has published over fifteen hundred works of nonfiction, most notably his first book for writers, *How to Get Your Book into Schools and Double Your Income with Volume Sales*, and also *Travis Roy: Quadriplegia and a Life of Purpose*. He has been honored with the Joe Concannon Hockey East Media Award and the Murray Kramer Scarlet Quill Award.

Visit him online at www.hendricksonwriter.com.

A Special Request from the Author: Word of mouth is

crucial for any author to succeed. If you enjoyed this book, please consider leaving a review where you purchased it. Even if it's only a line or two, it would make all the difference and would be very much appreciated.

For more information
www.hendricksonwriter.com/
david@hendricksonwriter.com

facebook.com/davewrites